STRANGE IRISH TALES FOR CHILDREN

STRANGE IRISH TALES FOR CHILDREN

EDDIE LENIHAN

MERCIER PRESS

MERCIER PRESS
PO Box 5, 5 French Church Street, Cork
16 Hume Street, Dublin 2

Text © Eddie Lenihan 1987
Illustrations © Joseph Gervin 1987

ISBN 0 85342 833 6

A CIP catalogue record for this book is available from the British Library.

14 13 12 11 10 9 8 7 6 5

Printed in Ireland by Colour Books Ltd.

Contents

Foreword

Reader, have you ever wondered what kind of Ireland it was that St Patrick worked in? Have you ever considered that he might have met Fionn Mac Cumhail, might even have asked his help in converting the Irish people to Christianity? There are those who say that this could not have been so, but they have not proved it. I say that it could have been so, and the stories in this book are my proof.

And what about the druids? No one, surely, will argue that St Patrick did not meet them. But what kind of men were they? Nowadays it is the fashion to dismiss them as some kind of magicians or charm-setters, but they were much more. They were the wise men, the educated few of their time and Patrick must have seen this very clearly, since he was nobody's fool. In fact, he must have struck up friendships with quite a number of them. To have been their enemy would have made his work very much more difficult, and surely not even a saint needs any more difficulties than he can handle. One thing is certain: the druids did not disappear overnight like the snakes. They practised their skills as always, but as the new religion grew in strength these skills were needed less and less and gradually they died out.

In the following stories there is fiction, of course, but since no one will ever know exactly how the past was, you are free to imagine that the adventures described here might really have taken place. As long as they take place in your mind I am happy at a job well done.

Edmund Lenihan

How the First Blackbird came to Ireland

In the days when Fionn Mac Cumhail and the Fianna were in the peak of their health there was one thing that every man had to be able to do when he was invited to a feast, and that was to stand up and entertain the lord of the house and the other guests. Every chief had his bard and harpist, of course, but the rest of the amusement during and after the feast had to be provided by those who had been invited. After all, what kind of thanks would it be to a lord to sit down for a whole night, filling yourself up with his good food, without being prepared to do something in return? And what good would it be to go to a feast where there was nothing but eating going on all around, and no singing, dancing or rhyming to help the food on its way down? Any warrior with any respect at all for himself would rather be whistling in the rain at the crossroads than at that kind of feast.

Now, one windy night, Fionn and three of his men, Goll Mac Mórna, Diarmaid Ó Duibhne and Conán Maol, were travelling the roads of Ireland and, indeed, at the time the roads *were* bad. They were jumping from pothole to pothole along a winding boreen when suddenly out of the gloom ahead they saw a light.

'Haaa!' cried Fionn, 'that might be a place where we could throw ourselves down for the night. We'll go

9

to the door and see what class of a welcome we'll get.'

At that time any man who had no welcome for Fionn and the Fianna would need to have a good excuse ready or he was liable to be wandering the roads himself a short time after refusing them. The first time they'd knock at the door; if a second time was necessary they'd knock it, in around the house, too. They were wild times in Ireland!

So, when they rapped at the door of this dún on this cold night, and the people inside saw who was there, they said: 'Come in, and welcome. Why didn't ye come sooner. We just needed the likes of ye to liven up our feast.'

They went in, made their greetings and sat down. Food was brought, and that food was of the best, which surprised them because it was a poor part of the country they were in. But they made no comment, only fell to it. So the feast went on and the music started. All went well for a while. Men ate heartily and ate enough while the man with the harp played sweet tunes. But a time came when his fingers got sore, his voice hoarse, so he put aside his instrument and fell to eating too. This was the signal for the man of the house to call on one of the guests to get up and do something to keep the crowd happy. His eye wandered over all the old familiar faces and his nose twitched in distaste as he realised that he had heard all their bad poetry, rasping voices and poor acting many times already. His gaze stopped at Fionn. There was a worthy candidate. He beckoned. At once Fionn stood up, knowing well that as chief guest all attention would be on him. Never would he have it said of him-

self or of any member of the Fianna that he put his
appetite before his duty to his host. He settled himself
in the middle of the floor and began to recite a long
poem which he had composed that very day while
walking along the roads. And he spoke it out in his
fine sounding voice, all about great deeds and three
battles long ago that his grandfather had fought
against four nests of giant spiders in the corner of the
kitchen of the Black House of Féitheacha Daoil. He
kept the feasters laughing and crying in turn for two
solid hours, and no man in that company told him to
hurry up, or to finish, that he was keeping them too
long from their food. When he *did* sit down they
nearly rose the roof clapping him and shouting for
'More! More! More!' But Fionn said: 'Hold on! Give
my voice a chance, good people. I need a bite to eat
now. I'm hungry from all that poetry. Let someone
else take up for a while.'

Diarmaid, famous for his good looks and strength,
was next to be chosen. Every inch the ladies' man he
was, but no mean man in battle either. Men who
taunted him on his good looks – and there had been
a few so foolish – were broken wrecks of their former
selves now, so when he walked to the centre of the
floor the onlookers avoided that subject and asked him
to do some mighty deed of strength there and then to
amuse them. No man more able to do so than Diarmaid! The hardest thing in the whole world to do, he
did it. Catching the straps of his own sandals,
'NNNNNGGHHH!' he lifted himself up into the air to the
height of a man's shoulder. Yes, by the straps of his
own sandals! Feet twitched and squirmed under

tables as men gaped in wonder at this mighty deed. And when he broke the spell by letting himself down with a mighty gasp they clapped him until their hands grew sore and pieces of mortar began to fall from the walls, so great was the noise. They looked at each other in awe, then called the servants to fill the goblets to relieve the excitement. Having drunk deeply the chief called for quiet again. He was enjoying himself thoroughly. All this new entertainment! It would provide food for talk months from now.

'These men are professionals indeed,' he began, 'and nothing makes me wonder more than how the next man' – and his eye fell on Conán Maol – 'is going to keep us amused after what we saw already.'

A nodding of heads, and a muttering of voices, 'True! True!'

Conán stood out, bowed, and began to sing, a sweet soothing song, in a voice that was neither loud or rough – a wonderful thing in a man that was *very* loud and rough. And how wonderfully he wove the song, all about walking through woods in frosty weather when the tracks of wild boar are clear on the ground.

Certainly, it crossed the minds of a few of his listeners that there was something odd about the words. . . 'Sure, wild boars make no tracks in frosty weather!' But he sang it so convincingly that those hearing him would have believed it if he said that every one of the same wild boars had six legs. And in any case, who in his right mind would interrupt a guest? Only an ill-bred lug would do a thing like that. So they sat there, their chins resting on one hand, drooling out of the corners of their mouths with pure interest and forgetfulness, so hauntingly did he sing. When he sat down there was no sound or movement out of the audience for a few seconds, until suddenly they seemed to wake up and a murmur went around the hall. 'O, boy,' they all said, 'wasn't he a singer an' a half. The training wasn't wasted on him, whoever his teacher was. Wasn't he the man that could put you thinking of your young days, walking through forests! Oho, I tell you, these fellows of the Fianna are no daws!'

The fourth member of the Fianna there, Goll Mac Mórna, was on the point of being called to do his piece when 'BANG! BANG! BANG!' knocking was heard at the door outside.

'Well, blast it!' snapped the lord of the house, 'isn't it the time they come disturbing us and we just enjoying ourselves highly. But go down anyway, someone, and see who's there.'

A servant went out, opened the door, and in stepped an old man with a grey cloak wrapped tightly about him. The poor devil, it was obvious that he had travelled for miles and miles because he was covered with dust. In his hand he grasped a staff, very like a crozier except that the head was undecorated. No doubt it was to help him over the rough roads and the rocks, so that he wouldn't fall down and break his knees.

He was brought in. He walked slowly up the hall, all the people watching him; naturally enough they were curious. He halted before the chief's seat at the top table, bowed down to his lordship and said:

'I claim my right, as a traveller this night.'

'And what might that be?' said the chief.

'A small bite to eat and a fist of straw in the corner,

14

if you can spare as much, good sir.'

'You're welcome! You're welcome! And d'you know what, if you were here a small bit sooner you'd have got some of the finest entertainment we ever had in this area. But you're not too late yet. There's more to come shortly. So be seated, and have what's going.' He ordered two servants to bring him something to eat, which they did at once.

However, the old man was soon forgotten because Goll was now called on to do his piece. Taking one last drink out of his goblet of poitín and wiping his mouth on his hairy arm he stepped out, loosening his dagger and sword as he went. Then, carefully, he wedged the sword-point down between two flagstones, stood back, balanced the dagger in his right hand and WHHHHHSSHH!! threw it at the sword. It struck the cross-beam of the handle and sprang back. At once, all the watchers ducked their heads into their hands, not knowing where it might land. But when they peeped out from behind their fingers a few seconds later there stood Goll with the dagger in his hand, looking very disgusted indeed. To think that he had just done his favourite trick, and that there was no one to watch it except the men of the Fianna, who were sick of seeing it performed!

'I thought ye wanted to see me doing my party-piece,' growled Goll.

'We're sorry for doubting your skill! It won't happen again,' they all chorused, very embarrassed. 'Please do it for us again. Just one more time.'

So he did, threw the dagger and caught it on the rebound with his bare hand. What could they do but clap and make all the noises of admiration? Three men were not clapping, though.

'It wasn't for that deed that you were accepted into the Fianna,' said Fionn, sitting casually, his hands folded over his stomach. 'You can surely do a bit better.'

Every eye swivelled towards Fionn. Men could hardly believe their ears.

'Better than that? What's the man raving about?' they whispered.

'I can, maybe,' replied Goll, a very modest look on his face.

He stood back from the sword again, let fly the dagger – WHHHHEEEUUU!! It hit the sword at the dead centre of the handle again, flashed back, and in that fraction of a second Goll stepped nimbly aside, opened his mouth and snatched it out of the air with his teeth. He bowed to the crowd, smiled, collected his sword and sat down.

The roof and walls shook with the mighty sound of clapping hands and stomping feet. It was like thunder. Deafening!

'Stop! Enough!' roared the chief over the din, and as the noise subsided he said, 'I'm not trying to make less of that great show, but we'll be without a roof over our heads if ye don't take it easy.'

Men returned to their drink and meat, but they continued to speak with admiration of Goll's feat. 'Is there another man in Ireland that could do it?' they said.

'Wouldn't it make your teeth water even to think of it!'

The feast went on quietly then for some time as

heartbeats returned to normal after the excitement. But one of the servants, leaning over the lord's shoulder to refill his goblet, whispered in his ear, and 'Oho!' breathed the big man, 'we were forgetting about yourself, my good fellow,' looking in the direction of the stranger who had lately come in. 'We're sorry about that. Every man deserves his chance of doing his little bit. Come out here, now, and do something for us. Anything that takes your fancy at all.'

The old man darted glances around but he made no stir to get up. He looked very frightened.

'No insult meant to the house, but I'm no good in front of a crowd,' said he.

'Get up, and out there on the floor!' snarled the lord, a very threatening look on his face. 'Is it trying to destroy the old custom and disturb our whole feast you are?'

'Indeed, I'm the last man in the world that'd do that,' whined the old man. The lord scowled at him.

'What would ye like him to do, men?' he cried, 'when he won't offer to do it himself.'

'Whistle!' shouted someone, and the whole hall took up the cry, 'Whistle! Whistle! Whistle!', while they hammered the tables with their daggers and fists. The old man looked like a hunted hare now, not knowing which way to turn.

'I can't whistle!' he protested, 'I can't do it, I tell ye!'

There was silence. That any man would refuse to do a little bit of entertaining, having taken the hospitality of the house! Oh, that was something they had heard about only in stories of the times when men were savages! Who was this unnatural wretch, at all?

17

'So, you can't whistle, hmm. Are you refusing to do it?' asked the chief grimly.

'No! No, I'm not!' croaked the old man. 'But look!' – he opened his mouth wide – 'Not a tooth in my head! How could I whistle with them two bare gums?'

'Whistle! Whistle! Whistle!' went the crowd behind him.

'That's the drink talking,' murmured Fionn sideways to Diarmaid. 'These boys are getting a small bit out of hand. It could get rowdy here tonight yet.'

Diarmaid nodded, his fingers drumming absently on the table. 'That's what I'm afraid of too.'

The chief was speaking again now.

'Take him out there to the carpenter,' he ordered, 'and he'll hammer a few timber pegs into his jaws an' they'll do for teeth.'

'Nooo! No! No!' wailed the old man, and he made a frantic rush for the door. But SSSKWISSSHH!! The two guards standing there crossed their spears in his path and barred his escape.

'Bring him up here!' shouted the lord, excitement in his voice.

Fionn rose now. This had gone far enough.

'Hold everything, there,' he said smoothly, stepping forward. He had never liked to see the old or the weak mocked. He was not going to start now.

'Wait a small minute, now! Lord of the house, myself and my friends here are very thankful for your hospitality and your food this night, and very glad to think we pleased you. But, since this man can't whistle like you asked him to – an' I'm not questioning your right to ask him to whistle – you won't be dishonouring your house if you let his place be taken by someone else. Would it please you to allow that? We, who entertained you so well – you admitted that yourself – we'll take this man with us, and I give you my word that within three weeks, no more, no less, I'll be back here and I'll have something to whistle in his place.'

'We'll take no one but himself. . .' spluttered the chief. But he saw the cold hard look in Fionn's eye and added hurriedly, –' except, of course, 'tis going to be something special entirely.'

Fionn relaxed a little. The danger-point had passed.

'Special is what it'll be,' he said pleasantly. 'Have you any reason to doubt us from what you saw already?'

They had no answer to that.

'All right. Three weeks. Be back here by then,' snapped the chief, trying to salvage some of his lost dignity. Fionn bowed slightly, turned, and strode between the silent tables to the door. Diarmaid, Goll and Conán followed, leading the old man before them. There were no farewells. The door snapped shut behind them and they were in the dark night again.

As they picked their way carefully down the narrow passage from the fort many thoughts chased each other through Fionn's mind. Something. . . something nagged at him but he could not pin it down. At last he could stand it no more. He stopped, laid his hand on the old man's arm and said:

'Well? Are you going to tell us your story? I have a feeling that I saw you somewhere before. Or you remind me of someone.'

19

'I might, indeed,' said the old man mildly.

'You're no ordinary travelling man,' said Fionn.

'That's true enough. Wasn't I on my way to see my brother, Taoscán Mac Liath, when the darkness fell on me and I had to call to that cursed place to look for shelter. I'm not as able as I was one time for sleeping under whitethorns or on the rough heather.'

'That's where I saw the face! Sure, you're the spitting image of Taoscán! Well, well! Isn't the world a small place, too, when you think of it. An' you're going to Tara, you tell me? You can come back with us, so, because that's where we're going. We'll show you where he is.'

'Oh, I know well where he is.'

'You do?' said Fionn.

'Why wouldn't I? I'm a druid like himself.'

'A druid. . . like. . . himself?' Fionn replied faintly. His tongue could hardly get around the words. 'An'. . . isn't it a strange thing, that with all the power you have, you couldn't do the bit of whistling they asked you to do! And here am I now, having given my word that I'd be back there in three weeks' time with something better, wherever I'm going to come by it.'

'Acting for a crowd was never a part of my studies, Fionn Mac Cumhail, and I'm a bit old to learn it now,' he replied icily. There was pride in his voice and something else. Something touchy.

Fionn decided that nothing could be gained by pressing the matter. Yet his annoyance grew, as they walked on, at the thought of the fix he had got himself into and he burst out, 'surely to heavens there was some place you could have pulled a few notes out of,

20

a man of your power. And what'll I do now?'

'Maybe there's more to this than you can see yet. We'll go on to Tara and see my brother first thing, that's what we'll do!' snapped the druid, ending all further discussion of the subject and leaving Fionn more mystified than before.

'More to this than I can see?' he snarled to himself. 'What I see is that I'm in trouble, that's all.'

They walked the rest of the journey in silence, until at last, as dawn was breaking, they came to Taoscán's cave at the foot of the Hill of Tara and went in.

Taoscán was his usual self, up and about even at this unheavenly hour, whistling like a lark as he prepared his first meal of the day. At the sound of the opening door he turned. His whistle died in mid-note and an expression of surprise and delight spread over his wrinkled old face. Three steps forward and they were wrapped in one another's arms, hugging, unhugging and slapping backs. Taoscán held his brother then at arms' length.

'Let me get a squint at you! Well, well. Where were you for the last six years? An' why didn't you write? Did you — ?'

His brother cut him off in mid-sentence.

'Oh, secret work. I'll tell you about it another time.'

They threw their arms about each other again. More hugging. And more. At last Fionn and the others became impatient as well as a little embarrassed.

Diarmaid began to make interrupting noises, 'Ahem-hem! Hh-hem! Eh-haa!'

Taoscán paused, turned to them and said: 'Is it so ye have sore throats? I told ye before, not to be staying out too long in the dark of the night in the mists and damp fogs. Ye'd want to stay at home more at night, men, because ye're getting a small bit frail in the health!'

They looked at each other in wonder. The fittest, the healthiest men in all of Ireland! Frail in the health, indeed!

'Look!' protested Fionn, nettle in his voice, 'will you stop talking nonsense, Taoscán! We brought your brother out of an awkward kind of a house a small while ago. Did he tell you what I have to do, though, with all his whisperings?'

'Don't I know it all,' said Taoscán. 'I'm not King Cormac's druid for nothing. You know that. I was keeping an eye on ye in the smoke of my fire. I saw the whole thing.'

'Fine,' said Fionn, 'but have you any words of help for me now?'

'I *could* help you. But better still, you could help yourself.'

'What's that?' demanded Fionn. 'Help myself?'

'You know your power, Fionn. You know your power.' Taoscán turned away wearily. How many times would he have to keep reminding him? At once Fionn brightened up.

'Well! well! I forgot entirely about it,' he smiled and put his left hand down into his oxter-bag, which hung securely under his right armpit. As always the bag served him well. The first thing that met his hand inside was a needle, which jabbed itself into his thumb.

'Wo-owwww!' he shrieked, jerking the injured

thumb out, up and straight into his mouth. But all was for the best, for this was the same thumb he had burned on the Salmon of Knowledge many years before, so the instant he put it into his mouth he saw a vision rise in front of his eyes, as if Taoscán had called it up out of the fire, a vision of a very, very stormy sea. Out beyond that ocean he could see land, with forests towering up out of it. Then he thought he heard the sweetest whistling ever heard by human ears, but it was a long way off and he could hear it only in snatches because the gusting wind was whipping it away. He strained to hear it more clearly, arching his neck in a gesture of pain so that Nathar Nimhe, Taoscán's pet snake, who was looking up at him from the back corner of the cave, thought he was gone clear out of his mind and scurried away to a darker and safer refuge.

In a little while the vision faded and Fionn came back to himself.

'Wha-! Wha-? . . . Taoscán, what land was that?'

'Oh,' said Taoscán, 'that's the land of Norway, Críocha Lochlainn, as the people call it themselves.'

'By Crom! Isn't that the place away, away up north where the big mountains of ice are floating around in the sea?' exclaimed Fionn.

'That's it, surely,' nodded Taoscán. 'And that's the place you'll have to go in order to get the greatest whistlers in the whole world.'

Taoscán's brother was looking in a knowing way at Fionn, but Fionn did not see that look. He was too busy trying to find out more.

'And what class of a thing was it that I heard

23

whistling so beautifully?'

'That was Lon Dubh, the black bird. He's the very one, now, that you must bring back to Ireland. And when you're at it, bring two of them. Two's better than one; you'd have more music morning and evening if you had two,' smiled Taoscán.

'I believe you,' replied Fionn. 'I'll go immediately,' and he wasted no time, but set off the same hour without touching food or drink, so charmed was he by the song of that creature of the cold north. Diarmaid, Goll and Conán groaned at the thought of more walking without a meal, but they snatched whatever was to hand and accompanied him as far as the Giant's Causeway. From there they looked out to the north and to the east. A storm was on the sea, just as in the vision. With thunderous roars the waves were smashing themselves into small pieces against the rocks, shaking the ground under the men's feet.

'By Crom, Fionn,' shouted Conán, trying to make himself heard above wind and wave, 'don't be in any hurry out there today or you'll get mangled off the rocks there.'

'What are you talking about?' roared Fionn also. 'I hear that music going around inside my ears, the sweetest whistling in the world. So I'm going.'

He said no more, only dived in while his men shook their heads. They had all been in love and in battles, so they knew how he felt. He surfaced, turned to them and yelled one sentence,

'Stay here and wait for me!'

So saying, off he went with huge powerful strokes, all his equipment on his back. For two days he fought the wild horses of the sea-god Manannán Mac Lir, sometimes on their backs, at other times smothered by their foaming breath. But his huge arms never stopped, the track of white spray behind him never died down until he came to the rocky shores of Norway. Only then did he raise his head out of the water, or clear the seaweed out of his ears. He clutched the black slippery rocks, hauled himself up and never rested until he found himself on the king's highway.

He met only a few people, but all were friendly enough and they all pointed him in the one direction: 'Go dat vay! Go dat vay!'

He did go that way, and almost before he knew it he was standing before a mighty dún, a great fort of bright stone, which obviously belonged to a king because a huge helmet with golden horns was painted up over the main gate and the doors were made of oak, studded with silver.

'Ah,' sighed Fionn, 'this is the place I'm looking for, all right,' and he banged on the thick timber with the Gae Dearg, his hunting-spear. The door was opened and he was let in. He explained his task to the king, Olaf Bandylegs, a friendly and sympathetic man, even though a horse and chariot could be driven between his legs, they were so bandy. Fionn said to him, 'Look, your highness! You know, yourself, the way 'tis. I got the nod that you have a creature in this country of yours that can whistle sweeter than any other in the whole world.'

'Oho! We have the very thing you are looking for, the lon dubh,' laughed King Olaf. 'But catch him you must for yourself.'

'That's the least I could do,' said Fionn happily. 'But where is he?'

'O, I'll show you. Come, up on the battlements, here.'

He led him to the top wall of the dún, pointed out: 'There below the wood is. In that place you will find him, together with all his family and friends. They are of no worth to us, because we hear them all of the time. In fact, they give us much trouble, singing at all hours of the morning when we would prefer to be asleep. So, please, take many of them, you hear?'

'Isn't it strange how they never came as far as Ireland,' said Fionn.

'The sea it is, maybe. It is long journey and perhaps they would be tired, so they stay here, eh?' said King Olaf.

'And 'tis only now I think of it, but why have we no singing birds at all in Ireland? The only ones I ever heard making any attempt at it are the crows. But we could nearly do without their kind of singing.'

'In that I cannot help you, I fear. But my druid will surely speak to you. He knows many things. Yes, and he gives me his thoughts on everything.'

From Olaf's resigned tone Fionn could guess that a long sermon was in store if he should meet the druid, so he thanked the king and hurriedly excused himself.

'Look, your majesty,' he explained, 'I'd love to be talking with that wise man, but I have to be back in double quick time to the land of Ireland. If I'm not I'll be shamed for ever and my word'll be worth nothing. So I'll make a start, if it's all right with you.'

'I understand your trouble,' said Olaf. 'I would not

like such to happen to ourselves,' so he sent Fionn off with his blessing, which was no small thing in those times. He said: 'May the luck of Odin go with you, brave man. But come back one day to see us when time is with you.'

'I'll do that,' said Fionn gratefully, 'and if there's any bit of a good turn I can ever do you I hope you won't be shy about asking.'

He was shown out and he rushed to the forest as fast as his feet would take him. He hardly had stepped under the dark green branches when he heard a delicate whistling over his head. He crept up close to the tree, and there above him was perched a jet-black bird with a yellow beak, and another above that again on a higher branch.

'By Crom,' whispered Fionn, 'he looks like an oul' crow that got his face stuck in sour butter. But no matter! He's the lad I want.'

He edged his way up the tree until he reached the branch where the first bird was. Slowly he inched his hand towards it.

'Come to daddy! Come to daddy!' he wheedled in his Sunday voice. Further and further he stretched his fingers but the bird always skipped just out of range. Fionn was losing patience now. He made a grab for his feathered tormentor but in doing so almost lost his grip on the tree-trunk. With a wild screech his two arms clutched the rough bark and he was safe for the moment. But the birds were gone, fleeing for dear life, their frightened shrieks echoing through the forest halls.

'Ah, blast it, come back!' shouted Fionn. 'I haven't

all day. Come here!' No chance of that. They led him around the woods for hours, over and back, from post to pillar, and he might still be there but for the tiredness that came on him, forcing him to sit and think. As he struggled to catch his breath, a light shone somewhere in the darkness of his mind. He smiled.

'Hah! I'm not going to be here all my life like a fool after ye, boys.' He put his hand into the oxter-bag, carefully this time, groped around and drew out a net, neatly folded.

'Heh-heh-heh!' he cackled. 'And isn't that the very thing I wanted badly.'

Filled with a new energy he began the chase again. The two birds were watching his every move now, trying to see some reason why this big mad fellow should be running around chasing them! So they kept well ahead of him, out of his range.

'By the hand of Lugh', wheezed Fionn, 'I'm no better off now. I'll never get close enough to throw the net.'

He looked at it. In his huge hand it looked harmless, almost useless. As if to agree with this opinion, the birds began to chitter. To Fionn's ears this sounded dangerously like mockery. He glared, gritted his teeth and flung the net in their direction, with – 'Yah! Ye horrible beasts! If I get my hands on those scrawny necks —' His threat was never finished. All his attention was fixed suddenly on the net, for it was changing as it flew through the air, growing bigger and bigger, spreading wider and wider.

'Dar Fia,' he cried, 'I should have known that it wouldn't be any ordinary thing that'd come out of the

oxter-bag.'

The birds had seen the danger by now and were fluttering every feather desperately in their efforts to escape. But it was useless. They were too late. The net had covered the whole tree where they were perched. They were trapped, as surely as if they had been in a cage. They flapped, they squealed, all the more so when they caught sight of Fionn like a great cat clambering up through the branches towards them. Fiercely they pecked and jabbed at his hairy fingers as he gently caught one and then the other in his big fist. Fionn felt nothing of this, only scrambled down, pulled the net after him and stuffed it back into the oxter-bag. Then, whistling a happy tune, he steered himself towards the sea and home.

He soon reached the shore, the birds still trembling in his grasp. But there he scratched his beard, perplexed.

'O! What'll I do now? I can't swim with these lads in my hands.'

He sat, took off his helmet to allow his brain to cool, and as he fingered the warm metal an idea came to him. Why not put the birds into the helmet, clamp it back on his head and tie it securely with two plaits of his long hair? He was pleased with his cleverness.

'I'm sorry to put ye in the dark like this, birds,' he said softly, tickling the frightened heads with his forefinger, 'but it won't be for long.' He was right about that, at least. With a last parting look at Norway, a short prayer to Manannán, he waded from the shore and was soon beating down the waves on his way back to Ireland. Hour after hour his strong arms brought him nearer to the coast of Antrim and when at last he saw the Giant's Causeway he could just make out the figures of Diarmaid and Conán seated, their heads down, very intent on a game of chess while Goll hunted for seals among the rocks. Conán was just about to make one of his better moves when a piercing shriek rang out. Goll had been leaning forward from a great rock, thinking he had seen a seal, when up out of the depths, covered with seaweed like a sea-monster, came Fionn, snorting and shaking water out of his ears, eyes and nose. Goll leaped back, collapsed among the jagged rocks. Conán was first on the scene. He almost doubled up with laughter to see the pitiable state of Goll, who was only now picking himself up.

'Blast your hungry self, Fionn! Is it trying to give me a heart-attack you are?' snarled Goll.

But his complaints went unheeded. The others were frantically questioning Fionn now: 'Did you get — ?'

'What have you — ?'

'Hold on! Hold on! Will ye give a man a chance to get his breath,' he wheezed, shaking small crabs, herrings and other surprised sea-creatures out of his hair and beard. Then he sat down, sighed with honest tiredness, and asked: 'Have any of ye a bite to offer me?'

'Dhera, don't mind that now! Can't you eat some other time. Did you bring back what you went for?'

'I did,' said Fionn.

'Well. . . where is it?' demanded Conán.

'He-he-heh!' chuckled Fionn. 'You can be amusing yourself guessing on the road back to Tara, now.'

31

They gave him a crust of bread and a lump of goat's-milk cheese and amid much protesting and begging, Fionn set off southwards.

'Aw, come on, Fionn. Show him to us, will you,' pleaded Goll.

'Is it that you'd want to put yourself before King Cormac in the seeing of him?' asked Fionn in a more sombre tone. He was getting very sick of all this badgering.

That finished their questions, but it didn't stop them wondering where the noise was coming from when the birds began to sing under Fionn's helmet. By the time they got to Tara they still had no idea and it was driving them frantic. Fionn left them in the courtyard, their curiosity all unsatisfied, and hurried off up to the king's private chambers. All royal engagements were cancelled for the rest of that day and neither Cormac nor Fionn were seen again until nightfall. Locked away they were, listening to the birds singing for hours on end.

At the feast that night everyone was in a frenzy of excitement because word had gone about that Fionn had indeed brought back the greatest whistlers in all the world and that nothing like them had ever been heard before. The occasion was marked by a special ceremony: Cormac in brand-new robes, Fionn wearing his best golden helmet.

All were seated and the feast began. But little was eaten. The excitement was too great for that. Finally Goll could put up with it no longer.

'A thiarna, Fionn! Is it trying to torture us you are? Will you show us the whistlers, you cruel man!'

Fionn glanced at Cormac, who nodded, smiling. Slowly he raised his hand and lifted the golden helmet. But if he expected a flood of song to fill the hall he was disappointed. Everyone stared, leaning forward in their chairs to look, their mouths open, for there nestling in Fionn's hair were four delicate blue eggs. The blackbirds had nested on his head! He did what anyone in the same position would do, put up his hand to find out what was there. But his fingers froze in mid-air at a shout from Taoscán, 'Keep down that hand, Fionn! Don't you see what's after happening?'

'I don't. But I can guess,' Fionn groaned.

'They have their nest made above in your hair. A great honour for you, surely. They like you!'

'Like me, is it? How am I going to get a wink of sleep any night with them up there?'

'Bed?' said Taoscán. 'There'll be no more bed until the four eggs are hatched out. Myself and my brother had enough trouble getting those eggs here, and we're not going to let a few sleepless nights ruin our plan now. But, sure, they'll hatch in no time in a fine warm place like that.'

There was no smile on Fionn's face to hear those words. So it had all been a plot laid by the clever druids. He had been used, without even being asked. He was about to spring up, no matter what anyone might say, but at that very moment the birds burst into song – they understood Taoscán's message – and that song charmed away all Fionn's anger, as well as the private worries of everyone else in the hall, too. Not another bite was eaten that night while the birds

were singing, and in the small hours of the following morning men stumbled out of that hall not knowing whether they were in this world or the next, they were so happy.

As for Fionn, he had to abide by the decision of Taoscán and leave the nest where it was. On second thoughts, it was the safest course. So, for almost two weeks after that he slept sitting on a chair with a guard at each side to make sure he did not collapse in the night. Even though he was exhausted, he was happy because the birds were singing for him constantly. In fact his head was nearly addled from it. But that did not stop him from keeping his word to the lord of the dún to which he had made the promise in the first place. As soon as the four eggs were hatched the nest was carefully removed and Fionn set off with the two birds in his helmet. When he released them on to the table in front of the lord of the house and they began to sing, all the men at the tables sat back; they were so delighted that they also forgot to eat their food. And that was no small matter, because next to fighting and hunting, feasting was the thing loved most in life by the men of Ireland.

It was too good to last, though. After exactly three minutes of this noble entertainment Fionn stepped in, picked up the birds and replaced them under his helmet. The lord rose in anger. A mutter crept around the hall.

'Look here, you! What's the meaning of – '

Fionn was already half-way to the door. He swung around.

'The promise I made here is kept. Even if it wasn't,

these have to be getting back to their family,' and he tapped his helmet. 'If that doesn't satisfy ye, talk to King Cormac about it.'

And so he left them.

* * * * *

No birds ever had as much care and attention as those four little ones. They grew and grew and in no long time Tara was the envy of all Ireland for sweet song. The blackbirds swarmed around it in their thousands, and around Fionn Mac Cumhail too. For him they sang in a very special way, as though he were closely related to them. And in a way, one could say he was, since it was he who brought them to Ireland in the first place.

The Strange Case of
Seán na Súl

The day Fionn Mac Cumhail and St Patrick arrived
back on the coast of Kerry having settled their
business with Fathach Mór, King of Skellig, a messenger stood waiting for them, together with fifty men
of the Fianna, and all their hunting-dogs, including
Fionn's favourites, Bran and Sceolan.

'There!' said the messenger, stepping forward
smartly, handing Patrick a message. 'Read that.'

As Patrick's eyes skimmed over the lines that part
of his face which was not covered by his beard went
pale.

'Oh! I knew it! Just what I expected, only worse,'
he cried.

'Huh? What is it?' demanded Fionn. 'Tell us.'

Patrick took no notice, only read on.

'Hi! Are you going to tell us at all what's in it?'

Patrick looked up now, moodily.

'I have orders here,' he said, 'not to tell anyone what
it is until we're across the Shannon and into Clare.'

'But does that mean you won't be able to tell me
about it, so?' said Diarmaid, disappointment showing
in his every word. His summer hunting-lodge was that
year near Glin, on the edge of the Shannon river, and
there he had determined to stay until Lá Samhna.
Such a promise, made by a man of the Fianna, could

not be lightly abandoned, and since Glin was on the south bank of the river he would not be able to share in Patrick's news, whatever it might be.

'I'm afraid that's the way 'tis, Diarmaid,' growled Patrick. 'Orders are orders. Now, we must set out at once.'

They did so, and their marching feet ate up the miles with never a halt until they saw the big river stretching out before them. It was time for Diarmaid to make a decision. Could he go back on his word and go with them? All his instincts told him that he should, though he was reluctant to do so. It would be the first time. In desperation he turned to Fionn.

'What'll I do, Fionn? Advise me. Will I stay, or come with ye?'

'That's a decision for yourself to make,' replied Fionn.

'You're a big help! Sure, if I could make it I wouldn't ask you.' He turned to Patrick.

'You're the only one that knows what's in that letter, Patrick. Let you be the one to say. Is it so serious? Would ye need me?'

His voice was hopeful. Patrick recognised this. He turned to Fionn and they walked aside a little way.

'I think we should take him, Fionn. You know how handy he is with a sword. A better man you couldn't have behind you in a tight spot – and there could be a few of them in this,' pointing to the letter.

'I don't know! Our word is our word. I wouldn't like people to think that we promise something one day and unpromise it the next just because it suits us.'

'Oh, I agree with you fully,' Patrick soothed, but

added, 'still, there are things in this letter that might make you feel different, if you knew them.'

'All right! All right! I can see you won't be satisfied until he's with us. But if there's any bad effects out of it you can take the blame!'

Patrick might have made an issue out of Fíonn's attitude but he decided that the letter's contents were too important for any more delay and so he was full of encouraging words for Diarmaid. 'I think that this time – just once, you understand! – you might put aside what you have promised and come with us. We'll be glad of your company, I'm sure.'

Diarmaid was in a frenzy of delight and went off to organise boats for their crossing, a task that was soon accomplished. As they sailed forth, Patrick stood thoughtful in the prow of the leading boat, wondering how much he should tell the men when they arrived on the Clare shore. He had little time for decision, for as soon they were across, and when they were standing in the Clare mud at the water's edge he gathered them all around him and read from the letter:

'Patrick, you holy man! Get Fionn Mac Cumhail and whatever help you can, and hurry to our assistance. Aid us quick or there won't be one of us left to tell the world about the terrible things that are happening in Tuath Clae.'

Patrick stopped and looked around him at the faces of the men.

'There's more in it too, but that's as much as you need to hear at this time,' and he folded the sheet of parchment carefully.

'Well, what are we waiting here for?' barked Fionn.

'Come on! Every minute counts by the sound of it.'

Northwards they went, towards Tuath Clae, pounding the roads. The following afternoon when they came near to Liscannor they noticed that there was an eerie silence over all the countryside. Not a soul was to be seen and for the life of them they could not imagine where everyone was.

Patrick looked around him as he walked and Fionn was scanning the very horizons, his hands shading his eyes. There was no living creature moving near or far away.

'Are you sure that people used to live here?' asked Goll.

'Throngs of them! The last time I was hunting down here there was no counting them. More plentiful than rabbits, they were.'

'What could have happened to them all, so?'

This was the kind of conversation between them as they marched, and they began to get a little bit worried at the lonesome state of the place, with no other soul moving but themselves.

They held their course, however, and were crossing the river near Ballyvaughan when Patrick's eagle eye caught sight of a little withered man, old and with straggly white hair. He watched them closely as they waded through the water, his chin resting on his hands and his hands resting on a stick. Patrick hissed to Fionn, 'Hsst! Look at the fellow over there watching us. Don't make any sudden moves, though. Just keep walking and pretend you don't see him at all.'

'But I don't,' said Fionn. 'Where is he?'

'He's as grey as the stones. You'd never notice him.

But never mind. Keep going and pretend nothing.'

They were close on three-quarters of the way through the water, splashing away, when a voice from the old man caused all except Patrick and Fionn to jump with fright.

'God save ye! Where are ye going in this cursed place? Who are ye and where are ye going, I say?'

'By Crom, isn't he the man for the questions,' muttered Fionn.

Patrick explained their errand. Immediately the old man heard their names his eyes brightened and he whispered, 'My prayers are answered. Ye came! And you're Patrick, the man we heard so much about? This must be Fionn Mac Cumhail, is it?'

'The very man,' replied Patrick. 'And these are the men of the Fianna.'

'As fine-looking a crowd of men as my old eyes ever saw,' and tears began to fill his eyes and fall down his cheeks.

Fionn, looking down on the old fellow, decided to get to the point.

'What's happening in this country?' he asked. 'Where are all the people? Are they gone to a fleadh ceoil, or to a hurling match on the Islands?'

'They're gone to none of those things,' replied the old man sadly. 'I wish they were, but they're not. No, they're all stolen away to Tír na nÓg or Cill Stuichín or someplace like that, I'm not sure. All I know is that they're not in the land of the living. This day three weeks ago a strange-looking man came to our country with a box under each arm and his face hidden behind a long bandage. The people gathered in crowds to

41

SEÁN·NA·SÚL

watch him wherever he'd go and that was when the damage was done. As soon as he had their attention he'd put his hand to the bandage and wind it off slowly, chin, mouth, nose, up along. And when it came to where his eyes should be there was no eyes in his face, at all. Of course, the first question they'd ask – poor decent people, all of them – was, "What happened your eyes, poor man?"

'As soon as that question was asked he'd open one of the boxes he had under his arm and there were his eyes inside! And when those eyes looked at the people they froze to the spot they were standing on. All he had to do then was go round and touch each one of them with this small black stick from his pocket and they shrank down to the size of ciarógs (beetles) and the lad gathered them up and into the other box. He's travelling the countryside doing that, so now ye know why there isn't a living soul around. Seán na Súl they call him and he has the place emptied.'

No man standing there by the little river knew it, but Seán na Súl was collecting people to carry them off to a magic island away in the western sea, there to be made servants to the one who ruled that land. She was powerful and evil and she had no liking for the people of Ireland, as we will discover in due course.

The men of the Fianna stood around with their mouths open while Fionn and Patrick asked the old man the dreaded question, 'Where is he now?'

'I'll tell ye as much as I can. Is Aughnanure known to ye?'

'Many's the time I hunted foxes between the rocks

there,' said Fionn.

'Well, two men arrived at my door three days ago, footsore and parched, begging a drink of water as if the Morrigu herself was after them. From the lands of O'Flaherty they said they were, a place called Aughnanure. They said he was there catching people by the armful and they were on their way to Caiseal Mumhan for help from the king of Munster. Every day he carried off a box full of them, off over the sea to that land out there. And they'll never again be seen, by the looks of things, unless you, Patrick, and you, Fionn, can do something. My son and my daughter as well as all the people I knew are gone, and I'd be gone myself too only I was sick in bed at the time he came so I wasn't able to get a look at his eyes. Don't leave me here, the last of all my people in an empty land.'

'We'll help all we can,' Fionn reassured him, 'but how can we avoid being caught ourselves? I want no holiday on an island, magic or otherwise, especially when I can't see the way I'm going.'

'And I wouldn't blame you for that,' said the old man. 'But, Fionn,' he continued, holding Fionn's hand, now, pleading, 'will you try your best to get that box, and the other one too, away from him. Because if you capture the box with his eyes in it he won't be able to see anymore. Maybe then he'll go away and leave the world in peace.'

'We'll see. Now, show us the place where you live and we'll take you home.'

They did that and they said to him as they were leaving: 'We'll be back in a couple of days, with news, and maybe more.'

'I hope so. I hope so, indeed,' he murmured softly, leaning on his door-post, as they took the road north once more to find this weird creature, Seán na Súl.

They set their faces for the great lake of Corrib, skirted its marshy southern shore where a few poor huts marked the place where a large city would one day grow up. The huts were silent now. Not even a dog came barking to greet them.

'He was here before us, by the look of it.'

'By the long arm of Nuada, there won't be a person in this part of King Cormac's land if we don't catch up with him soon.'

Patrick nodded, but it was hard to know whether he was nodding in agreement or whether his head was merely keeping time with his determined strides. Conversation died in the dust of the track and they marched on, westwards now, following the declining sun of the late afternoon.

A single blackbird was twittering a lonesome song on an ash tree when Fionn finally held up his hand, his signal to halt.

'Go quietly, now,' he warned. 'The fort of Aughnanure is just beyond that small hill.'

Any equipment that might jingle was held firmly in place now and fingers tightened on spears as they stealthily climbed the little hill. One by one, as they reached the summit, they lay full length on the scrub and long summer grass and gazed ahead. There, strong and squat, on another low hill less than half a mile away, sat the fort. With an expert eye Fionn surveyed the ground, measured the distance they would have to travel to get to the wall of the fort. He spoke softly to Conán Maol, who lay beside him.

'We'll take no chances. Every man stay where he is. I'll send the dogs out first and if he's in there he might show himself. He'll hardly do an injury to them, surely.'

He was about to click his fingers as a summons to the dogs when Diarmaid, on his other side, nudged him urgently.

'Will you look at what's there at the gate!'

All heads were stretching forward now, all eyes peering at the open gates of the fort. Yet it was not the fact that the gates were open that held their attention, but the large bulky figure sitting cross-legged in the centre of the entrance. Through the gathering dusk they could see that his head was completely wrapped in a bandage and each of his hands was resting heavily on a box, one on each side of him.

'That's our man, surely,' whispered Fionn. 'But the trouble is, which box are the people in. If we open the wrong one first the eyes'll look at us an' that's the finish of us!'

'Who says we'll ever get a chance of opening even the wrong one?' said Goll.

'Does he ever leave them out of his grip, I wonder?' mused Diarmaid.

'T-anam 'on diabhal (Damn you!), he hardly carries them to bed with him.'

'We'll watch him tonight,' Fionn decided, 'and maybe we'll find out his weakness – if he has one!'

At that moment a movement caught their attention. Off to the right, on a small path leading round the fort and out of sight, two men came into view talking and gesturing as though in serious conversation. Every man of the watchers gritted his teeth as they came on, seemingly unaware of their great danger. Fists clenched in the long grass as if such a gesture might do what words could not. But still they advanced towards the gate and stopped only when they almost tripped over the sitting figure in the fading light. Fionn noted their startled pause, their gesture of surprise and sympathy for the bandaged face. No word reached his ears, but he could imagine what they must be saying: 'What in the walls of the world happened your eyes, poor man?' And then, as they watched spellbound, the bandage was unwound slowly.

'Crom help us, but those two must be strangers to this part of the country or they'd never be standing where they are now,' whispered Goll. No one had time to answer, for immediately one of the boxes, the one under his right arm, snapped open and a pair of glittering eyes lay there, glaring out. Before the men could utter another word they were frozen to the spot and Seán na Súl, finished the unwinding of his bandage now, reached into a pocket. He drew out what looked like a short black stick, touched each man with it once and like a flash they shrank to the size of mice. With a low, evil cackle Seán na Súl gathered them up and swept them into the other box. It was open for only a few seconds but in that time Fionn and all his men heard the most pitiable cries from what seemed a large crowd of people, shrieks for help from poor souls who knew that they might never see their native land again.

'By the Gaé Dearg,' hissed Fionn, 'I won't sit here idle while that devil is taking all those people away!' and he made to get up.

'Easy! Easy!' cautioned Patrick. 'How do you know what other powers he might have to use against you? Anyway, don't you know enough now to free them all once you saw which box is which. So save yourself for later on. You'll get plenty of chances to fight before we leave this place, I'd say.'

Fionn could see the sense in Patrick's words so he lay down again.

His business now finished, Seán na Súl lumbered off into the fort and Fionn waited to see which window would light up. Sure enough, they soon saw the flickering flame of a fire in the darkness and they crept forward, up to the window. The wooden shutters were closed but through a chink in the boards Fionn could see all he wanted to. Seán na Súl was inside, just stretching himself on a bed of rushes in a corner and dragging a blanket up over himself while a fire of turf blazed away in the hearth.

'Isn't he fond of his comfort, the devil,' thought Fionn, his eyes taking in every detail. Then he saw what he most wished to know about: just inside the door, on the floor at the foot of the bed, he had put the box with the people in it. But the other box was on top of it, slightly open, so that the eyes could keep watch on the door all night to warn Seán of anyone coming in. At the first sign of movement they would begin to rattle loudly, enough to wake him, to do his worst to whoever was there.

Now he was settling down, the bandage back over his face, completely unaware, it seemed, that he was being closely observed from outside. Soon the noise of snoring was dancing from wall to wall of the room and nothing was stirring any more except the eyes glittering faintly in their box. Fionn let himself down gently and returned to his men. He said to Patrick, 'Tis going to be no easy job to get past those eyes in their box. They're at the door, on top of the other box.'

'He's no fool, at least. That's one thing sure,' replied Patrick stroking his beard in thought.

'The only chance is to come up behind it, snap it down, and one of us keep our hands down on it while the others sweep the box with the people out of there. But how'll we manage that?'

'By Crom,' said Diarmaid decisively, 'we'll have to think of something. We can't stay here all night just looking in at him sleeping, whatever else.' So they picked their way carefully to the gate of the fort. It was still wide open.

'That'll tell you how confident he is that no one'll creep up on him,' whispered Fionn.

'Will you stop, man! He'd be only too glad to see new customers for his box coming the way,' replied Patrick.

Into the empty, dark courtyard they crept, ears cocked for any sound. But there was no sound. Nothing only the thin hiss of their own breathing and the thumping of their hearts. In the shadow of the battlements they stopped and Fionn whispered to Bran and Sceolan, 'I want ye to go in there, lads, into the room where he is and see what ye can do. If ye could even knock the box with the eyes in it down on the floor ye'd be doing a great night's work. We'd do the rest after that.'

The dogs nodded and padded off down a gloomy passageway to the door of the room, Fionn and the men close behind. A huge iron bolt was fastened to the door but it was unlocked. Seán na Súl felt so safe that he never locked a door at night. Fionn fingered the bolt gently but that was the moment Bran chose to be curious. Nosing ahead he pushed against the door with all his weight. Fionn's grip on the bolt was not secure enough to prevent the hinges from moving, with a horrible creak. At once the eyes turned and rattled in their box, looking at the door. At the same moment Seán na Súl jumped up in the bed.

'Who's there?' he thundered in a floor-shaking voice, and then in the same breath, 'I'll have ye, so I will.'

He sprang out of bed, snapped up the box with the eyes and made straight for the door.

'Who's there?' he roared again as he gripped the heavy door to open it. Luckily Fionn had the quickness of mind to clamp both hands on to the bolt outside for dear life. Patrick was rattling, as violently as the eyes, in his sandals with fright.

'I know you're there, whoever you are!' bellowed Seán na Súl inside, giving the door a savage drag.

'Begor, we'd better be going,' screeched Fionn. 'I can't hold the devil.' Patrick, Diarmaid and the others stampeded back down the dark corridor towards the yard while Fionn gave Bran and Sceolan a last hasty order:

'Stay here, lads, and go for his legs when he comes out!'

'Rrrr!' they answered, and wagged their tails. At that growl the eyes inside rattled again, like marbles rattling around in an empty jug. Fionn suddenly let go the bolt to run as fast as he could, but at the same instant the ogre in the room gave an inhuman pull – and just as quickly landed on his back in the middle of the floor when the door came with him suddenly. With a snarl and a growl the two dogs jumped into the room, on top of him before he could recover, and the tussle started. From the shelter of a dark corner Fionn and the others could hear the confused din of battle, dogs snarling, Seán yowling and stamping, and the eyes rattling like some mad thing. It was music to their ears, though it would have been sweeter if they had dared take part in it themselves. Then they heard a loud snap and the rattling stopped at once.

'The box! It must have closed,' rapped Fionn. 'Come on! We'll chance it!'

He was at the room door before Patrick had even started to move. He stopped, peeped cautiously round the jamb, saw how things were inside and made a dash for the box where it lay on the floor. There was nothing Seán na Súl could do about it because the two dogs were at his throat, Bran sitting on his chest, Sceolan at his ear.

Fionn held the box tightly in his hairy arms and shouted, 'Patrick! Diarmaid! Quick! The other box, carry it out of here. Hurry!' Dogs or no dogs, when the man on the floor heard this he let a roar out of him and tried to get up. But Bran and Sceolan had not been trained by Fionn to keep down a wild boar for nothing. They squeezed their grip on him and quietened him again in a very short time.

Patrick clattered in, crozier in hand, Diarmaid behind him. They hoisted up the box on to their shoulders, clomped out the corridor and into the courtyard. At last, the two boxes were in their power. But for how long? Because now Fionn was finding it harder and harder to keep his part of the bargain. Drawing on some hidden power, the eyes were trying to break out of the box, and he could hear the muffled rattling inside rising dangerously. He grew frightened, but held on for his life.

'Are you safe, Patrick? Hurry on! These devils are trying to get out on me,' and he had to wrestle now to keep the cover closed. Only his mighty strength saved him: the eyes tired before he did. There was quiet for a minute, then he turned and said to Seán, who was still being closely guarded by the dogs.

'You, there! I have your eyes, and faith, I'll put them where they'll do no more harm, under water in the deepest hole in the river, or into the big fire at home, if you don't tell us where you came from and who you are. And you'd better talk fast!'

At the sound of Fionn's words, Seán na Súl grew very quiet for a moment. Then with a mighty push and a wolfish howl he knocked Bran back and stumbled towards Fionn, his fingers twitching for murder. Sceolan held on, though, and this gave Fionn time to jump back towards the fire.

'All right,' he snarled. 'No good trying to talk sense to you, so take this!' – and he leaped to the fireplace, pitched the box into the flames and stood motionless. The cover sprang open for the last time, the two eyes jumped out, into the fire, and a sudden shriek filled the room as if someone had had his face held in the flames by force. The eyes were screaming like living people! Then, WHHHSSSHHKK!! a blast of fire and smoke rushed up the chimney and at once Seán na Súl stopped struggling on the floor. Not a sound from him now. Tearing their gaze from the strange happening in the fireplace Fionn and the dogs stared at him, and there before their eyes he began to change from the big rough man with a bandaged face to a young handsome lad with wavy curling hair like Fionn's. And most astounding of all, he had two eyes like any ordinary man.

Sensing something here beyond their understanding the dogs, with yelps of surprise and fright, jumped back and sat growling at a safe distance, hair standing up all along their backs.

When he had changed fully into his new shape the man who had been Seán na Súl gaped up at them all.

'Where am I?' he asked, puzzled.

'*Who* are you?' growled Fionn in a rough voice.

'Who are *you*?' replied the lad. 'And these dogs, why are they growling at me?'

Fionn scratched his beard in amazement. But he was not half as amazed as Patrick and Diarmaid who were out in the yard listening to what was going on in the room when their box snapped open and people began to climb out of it. Surely, no such thing had been heard of before in Ireland – big people coming out of a small box! They were climbing over each

other, frantic, every one of them, to get out into the fresh air now that the spell was broken. The courtyard filled up with people and Patrick could only stand and watch, his mouth open. Never had he seen a miracle like this in all his travels.

One of the first to put his feet on the ground was a fine figure of a man, well-dressed and obviously used to getting his own way, because as other people struggled free of the box they kept respectfully behind him. It was the chieftain of the fort himself. He strode over to Patrick and said, 'You must be the one who saved us from Seán na Súl.'

'Well. . . amm. . . I. . . ah. . . I did my bit, but I'm not the man. Fionn Mac Cumhail, the man that really saved ye, is inside there in the room with that ugly fellow.'

'Draw every sword ye have, men, and we'll face him this time. A reward for the first man to sweep the head off of him!'

They rushed the corridor, as far as the door, but there they stopped in their tracks because the sight that greeted their eyes was not what they had expected. Before them stood Fionn and this handsome young man. Now it was their turn to gape as they crowded there, one behind the other, all pushing to get a look in.

'Where's Seán na Súl?' cried the chief at last.

'Here he is,' answered Fionn quietly, 'this young man here.'

'This is no time for jokes, Fionn Mac Cumhail,' said the chief. 'Where is he?'

''Tis no joke. This is him. But let him explain it him-

55

self.'

'I hope he can,' whispered the chief, looking a small bit doubtful now even at the sword he was holding. Then he said in a worried tone to the man beside him, 'D'you think are our wits gone astray from being inside in that oul' box?'

Before he could reply the young man began: 'A good many years ago, my father, the prince of Leacht Gheal, was having his dinner in his dún when this old woman came in looking for something to eat. She came up to his table and she said, "A small bit to eat, if you please. Spare a bit for me!"

'Whatever ailed my father that day, he had the bad word for her. He had a fierce temper always, anyway, my father.

'"Out of my dining-hall with you! We have no need of your likes here! I don't like the look of you," is what he said to her.

'"They're fine words, and fit for a prince, too," said she, mocking. "But from this day out you'll have bitter cause to use the like, because your son will find a big change when you and him least expect it. A changeling he'll be, a malartán (changeling), hee! hee! An' if *you* don't like what you see now, *he* won't see anything at all. You have my word for it!"

'With that, my father fell into a rage, a mighty temper, and he called his guards.

'"Catch that oul' cailleach (hag) and fire her out the door and let her be croaking her nonsense outside with the crows."

'They did. Flung her out in a heap on the road. But she shook her fist in at them and shrieked, "A malartán! A changeling! Don't forget what I said. We'll see who'll be laughing then."

'We forgot all about it, but I was out hunting in the forest one day about three years later when who should I meet but the same woman. She stood in the road in front of my horse and held up her withered old hand.

"'Stop! You're the young prince, aren't you?"

"'Move out of my way, dear woman," I said. "Let me go my road."

'I tried to get my horse to go on but she had some power over him. Not an inch would he stir.

"'You have no way only my way any more, boy," said she. "I know you well, and your father even better. Ye're a bad crowd, and I made ye a promise years ago, a promise I'm going to keep this day."

'With that, before I could move out of my saddle, she pulled out a wand, touched my elbow, and I was changed into Seán na Súl.

"'A malartán, indeed," she cackled.

'It was she who made me wander the country after that, looking for people and bringing them back to her island in the magic box. I had to do it. And if Fionn Mac Cumhail and his friends hadn't burned the eyes I'd be at it until the crack of Doom. She said to me when she sent me out the first time, "Your father didn't like what he saw, but that'll be no trouble to you because you'll see only what I want you to see. The eyes you have in that box, they're mine, and they'll watch over you until your task for me is done. And that could take a good many lifetimes, Hee! Heeeee!"

57

'When you burned those eyes, Fionn, the spell was broken and here I am now, safe and well.'

'An' I wonder what'll happen to herself?' said Patrick.

'That's a story that could be worth the telling, all right,' sighed the chief.

If they only knew it, she was in a bad way. When her eyes were burned by Fionn she gave a wild scream and burst from her room holding her face in her hands. For the rest of her days she was blind and wandered the world, groping along by the walls crying in a pitiful voice, 'Ohhh! Everything is dark. Where am I going? Where am I going?'

And shortly after, hundreds of people began to come ashore on the coast of Clare, wet and bewildered, but safe. Among them were the children of the old man of Ballyvaughan, and in a few days they were reunited amid great rejoicing.

The young prince, as soon as he had rested and recovered from his frightening experiences, went home, and of course his father was delighted to see him.

'Where did you come from?' he cried. 'We thought you were dead.'

'That's a story to be told over a feast,' said the prince, 'but here are the men that saved, me, Fionn Mac Cumhail, Diarmaid and Patrick.'

They bowed down to the prince of Leacht Gheal – 'Good day, and good health to your lordship.'

He came down from his throne, threw his arms around each of them in turn and planted a kiss of gratitude on their hairy cheeks.

'It is a great service ye have done for me and mine. If there is any request ye have, only say the word.'

Fionn or Diarmaid would take nothing.

'We were only doing our job,' they claimed. But Patrick asked if he might have permission to preach to the people in the prince's lands and convert them if he could.

'Don't mind this "if you can." I'll give the order myself and they'll all do what you'll tell them.'

Fionn and the son had no easy job convincing him that Patrick had to do the converting himself. The last thing they wanted to do was to make him angry again, knowing the temper he had. But they need not have worried.

'I'm a changed man,' said he to his son. 'I have a collar put on my temper since that time you were carried off, so talk away. And let Patrick do his own talking too, if that's the way he likes it.'

Oh, the relief they felt!

Being a ruler, though, and proud of his own generosity, as all rulers are, he couldn't let them depart with their hands hanging to them empty, so he gave Patrick a silver bell made by his own royal silver-smiths, and collars of gold to Fionn and Diarmaid.

Patrick made good use of that bell in converting the people of Leacht Gheal to the new religion, and ever afterwards, Fionn and Diarmaid wore their collars in battle, to dazzle their enemies and bring them luck. And they did.

Taoscán Mac Liath and the Magic Bees

In those far-off days it was the custom among people who had any little fortune at all to sweeten their wine, bread and almost everything they ate with honey. No such thing as sugar then. The poor man who had no money had no honey either and had to eat and drink whatever God sent him as it was.

At that time there was only one man in Ireland producing honey on a big scale, and that man lived down in Clonmel – it was called Cluain Meala then, the meadow of the honey. His name was Mel and he had a huge field crammed with hives, and every day the skies over a big part of Ireland were darkened by his swarms of bees as they came and went collecting the honey. The country people, making up the hay in the fields, would hear the buzzing coming, see the dark cloud and shout, 'Man, look at Mel's bees! He must be making a fortune out of them.'

Indeed he was, so much so that he was almost as rich as King Cormac himself. The money kept pouring in as the honey kept pouring out; in fact, he made his fortune while he was still a young man. But he made it honestly and no one could ever accuse him of short measure or poor quality. He sold only the best, honey fit for the High King's own table, and as a result that was exactly where King Cormac got his supply – and

everybody else who was anyone, too. It seemed that nothing could go wrong, and that the happy relationship between Mel and his customers would last for ever, but something happened to upset it.

* * * * * * * *

Once every year Taoscán Mac Liath would pack up his spell-books and a few other necessaries, wrap his grey cloak about him, and take himself off to the annual conference held by the druids of the Seven Lands. Sometimes the meeting would be held in Brittany, Scotland or Wales, at other times in Cornwall, Anglesey, the Isle of Man or Ireland and no business at home was so important that it could keep Taoscán from any one of those conferences. Not a single time in forty years had he missed one.

This year was no exception. He packed his newest experiments into his travelling bag and set out for that year's venue, which was the island of Rathlin, off the wild north coast of Aontroma. Lesser men might complain that in a forlorn place like that no work could be done, because with the cold Atlantic crashing against the cliffs and the wind from the north whistling around the shoulders of the hills no man could be expected to concentrate on deep magic, but the druids were no ordinary men. They needed solitude and privacy to accompany their secret discussions, and to get them they were prepared to travel even to the icy mountains of the northern horizon if needs be.

Now, the next stop after Rathlin is Iceland and that fact, maybe, explains why, that year, for the first time

in anyone's memory, there was a druid at the conference from Iceland. Taoscán, always alert, always
curious, was the first to notice his strange accent and
he was more than interested when he heard what he
had to say. Each druid there had to give a speech, tell
the others what new things he had been doing since
the last meeting. When the stranger's turn to speak
came the chairman announced: 'It now gives me great
pleasure to welcome, for the first time since the Big
Frost, a brother from Iceland. I present to ye Baldur
Barunsson.'

Of course – Clap! Clap! Clap! – they all gave him a
warm round of applause, and he bowed and began.

He spoke learnedly about carbuncles, and how to
get rid of them. He followed on wisely about how best
to clean drains in such a way as to get the water to
flow uphill. He lectured them on the use of butter to
prevent the axles of chariots from wearing, and on
how to stop the war-sandals of fighting-men from
squeaking so as to give no advantage to the enemy in
the dead of night.

'Oil of ze fishes iss all zat iss needed – und for ze
best results oil from ze noble land of Iceland.'

When the other druids heard this they were
inclined to take a dim view.

'The rules don't allow advertising, do they?'

'No, blast it. He should be called to order. And a
stranger too!'

But they forgot their unease when he began the last
part of his speech, all about bees. They could not take
it from him: he knew his bees! In fact, what he didn't
know about them the bees didn't know about them-

selves.

'My king in Iceland, he like bees. He have many bees and much honey he get from bees though there are not many flowers in Iceland. Ve have got secret to produce honey in big much from small land.'

As soon as Taoscán heard this he was all ears. He knew that if he could learn that secret and take it back to King Cormac there was no knowing what honours might be in store for him – maybe even a new consulting-room in the palace of Tara itself. It would save Cormac a fortune if he could get the huge amounts of honey a High King needed for his tables any other way than by buying it, so he was bound to be pleased.

Baldur Barunsson sat down when he had enough said. He had got a good round of applause, had bowed to the audience, and then, in the excitement of listening to the next speaker, everyone forgot about himself and his bees. Everyone, that is, except Taoscán. He kept a close eye on him and when all the speeches were over and they were on their way out to their dinner he cornered Baldur. They had the friendliest chat imaginable and the man from Iceland was so delighted to find someone as interested in bees as he was, and so proud to know so much about them, that it was only a very short time before a persuasive man like Taoscán had whatever secrets were in his head out of it and into his own.

A few days later he was on board a ship, on his way home, whistling to himself out of a happy heart. The captain of the ship scratched his head, wondered who this old lad was with the big grey beard, whistling all the time to beat the band. He thought he must surely be a runaway from the Dark House of Rorsgrunn or a scattered sage from the Forest of Muggendorf. But Taoscán cared not a weasel's whisker what anyone thought of him. He had the secret.

He came back to Tara with a light step, and still whistling, which made King Cormac and the men of the Fianna think that this was a usual homecoming from a usual conference, because normally when Taoscán got home the first thing he did was give his report. But this time was different. He went into his cave and left the welcomers standing about outside, looking at each other and shrugging their shoulders.

'Maybe 'tis the travelling that's getting him,' said Goll.

'Nothing to do only wait and see, I suppose,' growled Fionn.

They thought it all the more strange when they heard the bar being pulled on the door inside, especially since this was traditionally the time of open house at his cave, when he unveiled for them the new and wonderful things he had brought back from foreign places.

The day wore on, and at last King Cormac could stand the suspense no more.

'Blast it! Come on. We'll all go down and see what's going on. 'Tisn't like Taoscán to be acting in this strange way.'

Down they went, Cormac leading, and knocked at the door of the cave.

'Taoscán! Are you sick or what?' – No reply.

'Taoscán' – a small hint of impatience creeping into his voice now. King Cormac liked a prompt answer.

No noise for a minute. Cormac was just about to lose his temper when they heard, 'Bzzzzzz.'

They listened.

'What's that?'

'It sounds like bees, for all the world.'

'Bees! What would Taoscán want with bees inside in the house? Have you a bee in your bonnet?'

The sound of the bar being pulled back inside ended the argument there and then. They all turned to the door. It swung open and 'BZZZZZZZ!' out roared a swarm of bees.

'Ahh– ah! Arhhh!'

They were doing their best to scatter when Taoscán appeared and cried, 'Don't stir, men! Stand fine where ye are.'

The bees thundered past their ears and off in a cloud over the hill of Tara.

'Bless and protect us!' gasped Cormac, 'where did they come from?'

'Oh-ho-ho!' chuckled Taoscán. 'Come in 'til I show you.'

They trooped in, prepared for some unusual sight. But everything seemed to be as always.

'Well?' said Cormac, 'what is it you have for us?'

'This,' replied Taoscán, holding up a small bag, very like the money bags that travelling men hung about their necks at that time.

'What would you think that bag was for?' he asked Cormac.

'For your money, what else!'

'Indeed 'tisn't,' said Taoscán, distaste in his voice. 'And if I had any money 'tisn't here I'd keep it. There's

something far more important than oul' money here!
I suppose ye were all wondering why I came in home
instead of going up to give ye the good news.'

'Good news?' Cormac scratched his beard.

'About the bees! The ones that passed ye out the
door.'

At these odd words the Fianna began to fidget and
nudge each other.

'Oh, the poor man has a fever,' whispered Fionn to
Goll.

'Who'll we get as a doctor for the doctor when the
doctor is sick himself?' asked Goll.

'That's the bother,' replied Fionn.

'I heard what ye said!' thundered Taoscán, 'but I'll
let it pass. Lucky for ye that I'm in a good humour.'

That quietened them.

'But now, let me explain a few things for ye,'
Taoscán continued, his voice becoming quieter. And
so he explained to them how he had talked Baldur
Barunsson into giving him the secret of the magic
bees.

'They're living in that bag, and I can call them back
here any time I want to.'

'Do it now, so, 'til we see,' said Cormac, wonder in
his voice.

Taoscán took what looked like a little whistle from
somewhere under his cloak, blew two blasts on it –
Wheee-huu! Huu-wheee! – and immediately the
swarm of bees roared back into the cave, making the
men cringe. Then, one by one, into the bag they drop-
ped, thousands upon thousands of them.

Naturally enough, the men stared at each other, in

awe and admiration, also relief when they saw the last bee dragging his legs into the bag.

'Boys o' boys, that's a great trick entirely, Taoscán. But what good are they besides?'

'Am I talking to the men of Tara or to a pack of fools?' quivered Taoscán. 'Don't ye see! We'll have honey from this day out like no honey in the land of Ireland. That's what good they are!'

That was how it was. Every morning from then on Cormac had to send down two men to Taoscán's cave to bring up the honey on their backs – all out of the small bag, with no trace of a hive or anything else.

Time went on, and one night Fionn said to Cormac, 'Isn't it awful foolishness to be getting our honey yet from Mel, in Cluain Meala, when we have our own?'

'I know,' Cormac agreed, 'but we're doing business with him a long time and I don't like to finish it off without a good excuse.'

'Leave it to me,' smiled Fionn.

He went down the shiny stone steps to the store-room where the barrels of honey were kept, opened one of the two barrels standing there, stirred in a fist of dried herbs, put on the cover again and left, smiling.

Three weeks later, at a very important feast, where delegates from the king of Greece were being entertained, the sweetened wine was brought in, made from the honey in the two barrels. Needless to say, the herbs Fionn had added in the cellar were not guaranteed to improve the drinker's health, and they didn't, because everyone who drank the doctored honey-drink had to be excused early, bent double from cramps and pains.

Naturally, King Cormac was the outraged host. He sent for the kitchenmaids and threatened death on them if they had no explanation for the bad drink. However, those poor girls could only tell him that they had used the same ingredients as usual. He was just on the point of doing something rash when Fionn leaned across and whispered, 'Hold your hand a small minute, your highness. 'Tis the honey that's wrong, an' not the girls' – giving them a hairy grin.

'How so? Who told you that?' demanded Cormac.

'Look here' – pushing his goblet over to Cormac – 'what do you make of that?'

Cormac tasted it. Unsweetened wine, and perfectly good.

'Ho!' he roared. 'That villain Mel. Cancel our order with him this very night!'

Before dawn a messenger was riding hard towards Clonmel to give Mel the bad news, that they didn't want his bad-quality, watery honey any more, that they had their own, and the best, too!

Mel was not pleased to hear this.

'Oh, the devils! Are they setting up a company to rival me, put me out of the business?'

His first inclination was to cut off the messenger's two ears and send them back to Tara by separate post, but he thought better of it when his druid reminded him of the things Fionn Mac Cumhail and the Fianna could do to those who insulted King Cormac.

The world whirled on its way and things rested so. The fame of the bees of Tara spread and eventually people began to invite themselves to the court of the

King (since invitations were no longer being issued by Cormac) and did everything else short of breaking down the gates to get in to taste the honey. It got so bad for Mel that men who had been long-time customers began to say to him, 'Hi! That stuff you're selling is only pure súlach (juice). Is it out of turnips you're making it, or what?'

'Blast ye,' shouted Mel, 'while I was the only one supplying it ye thought it was fine stuff. Isn't it very pernickety ye're getting.'

The long and the short of the story was that Mel's business began to fail. So one night he sat down with his wife and his three big hairy sons and said, 'We're burst! Gone to the wall! And there'll be no living to be got here for any one of the three of ye if something isn't done about those bees above in Tara. Ye'll starve!'

'Dada, don't worry,' said Maolruan, the youngest son. 'I'll go to Tara and I won't come home with my hands empty.'

'You have my blessing,' sighed Mel. That counted for a lot, because whatever else could be said about Mel no one could deny that he knew all about bees. As did his sons, indeed. In fact they were often heard talking to the little creatures and no one thought it in the least odd since the results were there year after year to prove the value of it. But now times had changed and more than talk was needed. Maolruan took his road to Tara and arrived at the foot of the hill just as the sun was throwing its first rays on the water of the River Boyne. He went no farther, made no attempt to get an invitation; he had no need of it because he believed all the stories he had heard about

70

the honey. It was good stuff. No use in denying it. Instead, he picked a shady spot, low on the hill, but high enough to give him a clear view of all the country around. There he planted himself and waited with the patience of a man who realises that all depends on him alone. Sure enough, he was rewarded when, just before sunset, his keen eyes picked out a cloud lumbering heavily towards Tara. Moments later his ears, well tuned to bees' buzzings, detected the first hum of beating wings. But he was confused now. Having seen no bees leave Tara all day he could not, for the life of him, imagine how they could now be returning. Possibilities flashed through his mind, none of them satisfying, some frightening, while all the time the hum became louder, the cloud larger and darker. His eyes locked on them and followed them all the way to their destination – Taoscán's cave. As he watched, amazed, they streamed in through a specially-made little window in the side of the cave and vanished from his sight. He stirred himself, darted forwards, hunching his shoulders low as if to avoid being seen. At the window he eased himself up, peeped in but saw no trace of the bees. Stranger still, he saw no hive.

'Where in the name of Lugh are they gone? Or where does this lad keep them?' he muttered to himself.

If only he had seen the bag hanging down by the window he could have put in his hand and taken it, but how could he have known that the bees were in it?

'Oh! What'll I do now? I can't go home without the bees or we're destroyed.'

He considered his next move for a minute. Then

his eyes brightened and he stepped round to the front door and knocked. Taoscán came out.

'Good evening to you. And what can I help you with?'

'I'm in need of assistance, and in an awful hurry. Is there a druid in these parts?'

'There is,' said Taoscán.

'Tell me where, good man. My brother and myself were travelling to Tara when a rabbit frightened his horse and he got thrown near where the stream crosses the road. He can't get up and I'm afraid something is broken.'

As soon as Taoscán heard of someone in pain his face brightened.

'Hold on until I get my bag.'

He came back immediately and said to Maolruan, 'Take me to the place.'

'Would you. . . would you mind if I stayed here? I have a very weak stomach for injuries and I'd only be a hindrance to you.'

Taoscán looked hard at him but said nothing, only turned and went. He pulled out the door after him but didn't lock it, and as soon as he was out of sight Maolruan dived in, rooted around, but could find no trace of any bees.

'Damn and roast it!' he cursed, 'where'd he hide them?'

He looked up, down, high and low but could find nothing.

'Ah, to Hell with it! I must go' – because, glancing out the window, he saw Taoscán hurrying back, temper in every step.

Just as he was turning from the window he saw the bag and 'Begor,' said he, 'if I have nothing else to show for my trip I'll have his money anyway, the devil.'

He snatched the bag and ran for the door. Just in time! Because Taoscán stomped up, muttering and growling to himself about the kind of young blackguards going the roads nowadays. Maolruan stayed at the side of the cave, his back to the wall, until he heard the door closing. Then he ran down the hill and off towards Cluain Meala.

Taoscán only discovered the robbery the following morning. But when he did the lamenting started: 'Awww! Olagón-ó! My bees! My bees are gone! What's to be done? Baldur Barunsson'll put his curse on us all!'

However, that fit of hysterics lasted only a very short time. His training came to his assistance. He shook himself, poked up the fire to get the smoke rising and then added a pinch of vision-powder. Immediately in the smoke he saw Maolruan running along a road in the flat land near Cluain Meala.

'Oh, that scoundrel! He took advantage of my kindness. But he'll suffer for it.'

He went to his spell-book and called down black clouds and raging winds on Maolruan. It might have stopped another man, but Maolruan was near home now so he struggled on, especially since he guessed where the storm was coming from. He ran in the gate of his father's house, hailstones as big as duck eggs bouncing off the ground all around him. But he was safe – for the moment.

Mel was waiting for him.

73

'Did you get the bees?' he asked, excitement in his voice.

'I couldn't find the dirty things,' stuttered Maolruan. 'But, bedad, I got his money.'

'What good is his money to us, you bastún (lout)?' roared Mel. ''Tis the bees we wanted.'

'I'm sorry, but I saw them going into his cave, but that's the last I saw of them. There was no sign of them when I went in.'

'What kind of fool are you? Aren't you long enough at bees! Did you see the hives?'

'There was *no* hive there!'

'What ráiméis (rubbish) are you talking? Bees without a hive? Do you take me for a fool?' – snatching the purse from Maolruan's hands, swinging it, to strike him over the head with it.

'Sure, there's nothing in this purse, you simpleton!' He rattled the purse. No rattle.

'So that's your way of getting rich now! Stealing empty purses. Oh! What kind of a fool did I rear when I reared you?'

He pulled the string of the purse in his temper, and as soon as he did he heard the 'Bzzzzz!' He snapped it shut and in an instant his whole face changed. He knew!

'Boys, O boys! Boys, O boys, O boys!'

The three sons thought he had taken leave of his senses as he walked – nearly trotted – round the house muttering 'Boys, O boys, O boys!' to himself, keeping a tight hold on the bag.

But no one dared question him. At last he stopped.

'D'you know, in spite of yourself you're a great lad,

Maolruan. You did your job well, after all.'

Poor Maolruan had no clue what his father was talking about and looked with frightened eyes at his brothers.

'D'ye realise what's in this bag, here?' Mel asked.

'No,' said the three sons.

'The bees. The bees! Shhh! Listen.'

He loosened the string of the purse, and 'Bzzzz!'

'Oh, that's great, dada, but close it up, quick. They're hungry, and if they get out they'll murder us.'

He tied the bag and they held a conference.

'Aha!' laughed Mel. 'We have the winning of this battle here in our hands. All we have to do is keep these lads in the bag and soon Cormac and all our old customers will have to come to us again. But, begor, they'll pay well for their honey this time! We'll double the price and halve the supply. That'll teach them manners.'

There was just one problem: neither Mel nor his sons were used to managing magic bees, so they decided to put the bag down behind the bed and to forget they were ever there. They might have, too, except that the bed began to rise off the floor. The bees were busy inside and when no one was taking out the honey or when they couldn't come out to stretch themselves, naturally enough the bag had either to stretch or burst. Being made of the best of magic material it couldn't burst. But it could stretch. And it *did*. And stretched, out and out, until it filled the room. Only when they were going to bed did they discover it and by then it was too late to do anything.

'Olagón-ó!' cried Mel. 'We're ruined.'

And they were, because in no time the roof began to lift off the house, the walls cracked, buckled and fell to the ground.

'Oh! 'Tis the cold roads for us from this day out,' moaned Maolruan.

'We'd better go before worse happens.'

'And if they get out and follow us?' snarled Mel. 'No! As much as it breaks my heart to do it, we'll have to get that druid fellow from Tara down here to control them or the whole country, including ourselves, is going to drown. Maolruan, go back quick, like a good lad, and see can you persuade him to come.'

He went, protesting all the way. But he never got to Tara, because a mile down the road: 'Tramp! Tramp! Trammmp!' he heard the marching feet coming in his direction. He faltered, unsure what to do. Then, before he could make up his mind to run, he saw none other than the Fianna bearing down on him, fully armed for action and led by Fionn and Taoscán.

Maolruan fell on his knees, half from fright, half from relief, begged their forgiveness and their help all in the one breath, and was starting to explain about the terrible bag when Fionn silenced him: 'Don't be telling us what we know already! Taoscán Mac Liath followed it all in the smoke, and lucky for you that he did. Get up at once, and lead on home!'

Maolruan was overjoyed to do so and in a short time they marched into the yard of Mel's house, only to see the strangest sight ever, what looked like an overgrown bladder swelling and growing where the house used to be. Fionn was as surprised as any, but he had to show his authority, so he called out in a loud voice: 'Where is Mel, supplier of bad honey to King Cormac, and answerable for that crime under the laws of the Brehons?'

Mel stepped from behind a clump of bushes, a look of relief on his face. He let the insult to his dignity pass and spoke directly to Taoscán: 'Wise man, we did you wrong and we know it! But make allowance for our foolish ignorance, will you. Only take away the lads inside the bag and we'll do whatever you say.'

Taoscán was not a man without understanding or sympathy, and when he considered Mel's position – his business gone, his house in ruins – he thought he had suffered enough so he said: 'In spite of your wrongdoing, your disrespect and robbery, I'll take this no farther. But you'll –'

At that instant there was a loud commotion behind them, a cloud of dust from wheels and horses' hooves, and there was the High King himself, Cormac, spring-ing from his chariot, striding towards them – fresh from Tara to see the action for himself.

'Well, now,' said he, rubbing his hands, all business, 'are ye still standing here looking at each other?'

'The bother is to know what to do,' muttered Fionn.

'There's only one thing to be done,' grated Cormac, turning on him. 'One thing! Get that honey out of there, and don't spill a drop. Jump to it! I have import-ant guests coming tonight and they'll be expecting no less than the best.'

Fionn hesitated, lost for ideas. He looked hopefully at Taoscán.

'I'll try my spell-books,' he said, without too much

enthusiasm, 'but I'm nearly sure I have no spells for bees.'

He was right. He had none. They might be standing there yet had not Mel roused himself and said to his sons, with authority in his voice: 'Run to the barrel-shed and get the big tap!' and to the others standing around: 'Magic or not, they're still bees, and there's no man here that knows more about bees than me. So step back a piece, now, if ye want the job done right.'

His confidence was coming to him now that he saw other men at a loss; he was even beginning to see a way of getting back Cormac's business again. Maolruan came running back, tap in hand, and Mel set to work, whistling to himself all the while.

'He must be fairly sure of himself,' said Fionn.

'Is it my father?' answered Maolruan proudly. 'He can talk to the bees.'

'There's little hope for us if that's the kind of an amadán (fool) he is,' snarled Fionn.

Maolruan ignored that. His eyes were on Mel, who now took the tap to the neck of the bag, where it was tied, and began to talk to himself as the bystanders thought.

'Where are you? Come on out, now. You're going home. Come to daddy!' and so forth, with much buzzing and humming thrown in for good measure.

'If he hasn't bees in his bonnet I'm not Fionn Mac Cumhail. But I'll put a stop to him before he gets us all killed,' breathed Fionn.

'Will you stop and open your eyes! Look at the bag,' hissed Maolruan. Everyone else was already watching it. It had stopped growing and all the heaving inside had quietened. Mel was still buzzing, talking and rubbing one particular spot. He beckoned to Taoscán, who hurried to him.

'They want to go home,' stated Mel directly.

'Ah. . . Who wants to go home?' asked Taoscán, not quite knowing what Mel was talking about.

'The bees! The bees, of course!'

'Home?'

'Look! I'm talking here to the queen, and she just told me that they're lonesome for Iceland and they want to go back.'

'No such thing!' yelled Taoscán. 'What would Cormac say? He'd have our lives only to mention it.'

At those words a buzzing that sounded like a scream rose from inside and the bag began to swell again, twice as fast as before.

'Oh! Now you upset her. We're all doomed now, 'cos when the bag bursts they'll follow us to the four corners of the world,' moaned Mel in a hollow whisper.

Cormac, when he saw the bag growing again, strode up, questioned them, heard the bad news.

'Is there any other cure but to let them off home?'

'I'm afraid there isn't, your highness,' said Mel.

'Needs must when the Devil drives,' Cormac sighed. 'Do what you have to, my good man.'

'I'll do what I can – if they'll listen to me *now*.'

Mel set to work again and by a mixture of plámás, begging and promises he got the queen bee's attention. The bag stopped growing – big sigh of relief from the crowd – and in a while Mel turned and this time addressed everyone present: 'King Cormac, men of

Tara! The bees of Baldur Barunsson are lonesome for home, and surely, men, no fair-minded person would be prepared to stand in the way of such faithful servants as they have been during their stay with us! Are the men of Ireland such blackguards that they'd make prisoners of their friends forever?'

'No! No indeed!' shouted a fair section of the crowd.

'If we *don't* let them go,' said Mel, his voice changing to an ominous rattle, 'there'll be none of us here to talk about it, 'cos as soon as that bag bursts they'll have our lives! We'll look like hedgehogs!'

Silence.

'So, men of Ireland' – voice changing again, bright and jolly – 'we'll do the decent thing and let them go. And now, who's first for honey the like of which was never before tasted?'

As though a spell were broken, there was a mad rush forward, King Cormac included, as Mel stuck the pipe of the tap in the neck of the bag, loosened the cords slightly, adjusted the flow, and started dispensing, talking to the bees all the time while Maolruan kept the grasping hands at bay. Helmets, shields, scabbards, even battle-sandals, were passed forward to be filled, and no man was turned away empty-handed. And, oh! the strength of that honey! From being in the bag so long it was now fermented and as a result no poitín or mead tasted in the land of Ireland could equal it in strength or kicking-power.

The word spread, of course, and soon the people of all that district were flocking to the spot. Everyone got his fill, and still the bag was not empty. Soon, on Cormac's orders, the big barrels were brought from Tara and all through the night the work went on until there were no more barrels to be filled and Mel's hands were on the point of dropping off with tiredness. Silence fell. Even the guards placed on the bag by Fionn slept, and were well into their third dream, their heads full of delicious visions after the feed of honey, when a dark figure – none other than Mel – crept up to the mouth of the bag, opened the cord carefully and, crónáning and wheedling lowly, called the bees out. They came in their hundreds, thousands, and gathered all over the bag. Mel buzzed his final good-byes to the queen, gave his regards to all in Iceland and went back to bed, his good deed done.

Morning came, and the first notion that the guards had that anything was wrong was when a hubbub of voices penetrated their dreams.

'Where is it? When did they take it?'

The guards jumped up.

'Take what? Who are ye and what are ye shouting about?'

'We're here for the honey, but we don't see it. And we want to know why!' roared the people.

Only now did the terrible truth dawn on the guards. The bag was gone! They were guarding an empty plot of ground.

Ignoring the abuse of the crowd they packed their belongings with the determination of frightened men and marched for Tara, Mel with them. Arriving, they rushed past the sentries, called for Cormac urgently, but he was not to be found – sound asleep after the feed of honey of the night before. Relief flooded their faces and they mopped their brows.

they had the best of limestone feeding there, so their like was not to be had in the rest of Munster. Of course it was from there, and nowhere else, that Aengus Flúirseach used to get his supplies.

He had been getting eels for his feasts from Doolin for as long as he or anyone else could remember, and his father before him, so he had no intention of changing his plans now.

One May Day, he had invited a huge crowd, a noted and ferocious gang of eaters, to his palace, and many new eel dishes had been created for the occasion. The cooks had not been idle. Over the dark months of the winter they had slaved in their tall white thinking-caps and now a whole new batch of recipes had been invented to tickle even Aengus' appetite. He looked forward to the first feast of the new season with delight and pride in his skilful chefs.

'If your guests don't eat their fingers after these dishes,' they told him confidently, 'you can put us in charge of the stables instead of the kitchens.'

As the day approached all preparations were being made as usual and everything was going ahead perfectly. The cutlery was polished and the carpenters were busy planing down the tables after the last feast, and it seemed as if all was going to be fine. Every invitation had gone out and preparations were nearly made when a messenger came staggering into the palace, his clothes hanging in rags about him. He looked like a man who had just had a narrow escape from a pack of hungry wolves. The guards let him in, certainly, but no one was inclined to touch him. They were afraid of him. Aengus got word of it and the

Taoscán was called, and he it was who broke the news to Cormac in the comfort of his royal bed that the bag was gone.

'That puts no surprise on me,' purred Cormac. 'Didn't they say they weren't staying with us. Anyway, aren't the cellars full to the ceiling with their honey, and what more could you ask for?'

'True enough,' admitted Taoscán, 'but that won't last forever with the demand that'll be for it.'

'Hmmm!' Cormac thought. Suddenly he landed his two legs on the floor.

'Where is Mel? Get him and bring him before me at once!'

Taoscán shrugged, brought Mel into the royal presence and waited. Cormac was pacing the floor in his nightgown. He turned.

'Tell me! Are you good at mixing honey?'

'Me?' said Mel, looking around.

'Yes! Yes, you!' snapped Cormac. 'Well? Are you?'

'None better,' replied Mel proudly. 'I have my father's an' my grandfather's secrets.'

'Good, because I'm appointing you Honey Blender to the High King from this hour. Go down to the cellars and find the right mix of our grand Iceland honey with the ordinary stuff so that our visitors can still be satisfied while we spare the best.'

'I'll need to get a supply of ordinary honey, your highness,' said Mel. 'Have I your permission to do so?'

'You have. Go now and see to it!'

'And I know the very man to supply it, too,' he said to Taoscán, as he bowed and passed out.

A short while later Maolruan set up his own business out of the remains of his father's place, and being a capable young man he made a success of it in a short time. Certainly, the steady orders from Tara helped him, orders which grew and grew after the great discovery made by Mel in the cellars that no matter how small an amount of the special honey was mixed with no matter how big an amount of Maolruan's the quality remained pure magic!

After that father and son prospered. They had honour as well as wealth, the son being Royal Supplier, the father Royal Blender of Honey. They continued so till the end of their days, no one being the wiser about how easy Mel's job really was, and no one questioning him because there were just too many satisfied customers.

Fionn Mac Cumhail and the Making of the Burren

Long ago, there was a king in a part of Clare called Corca Baiscinn whose name was Aengus McNamara. But to all who knew him he was known as Aengus Flúirseach, or Aengus the Generous. That name stuck to him because he was a most open-handed man: the tables in his palace at Cathair Mhór, near Ballyvaughan, were never bare and his door was always open to everyone. One thing in particular he was fond of, and famous for, and that was eels. He would eat eels boiled, baked and jellied, in eel pies, eel cakes and eel sandwiches. He would enjoy eels any way his cooks might prepare them. So addicted was he that if the eels, for any reason, couldn't be cooked he would eat them raw. Maybe it was no more than a fad, but it made his reputation as a connoisseur of good food, and so his feasts were always booked out at least three years in advance. Women used to sell their jewels and men their armour only to be allowed to come and watch from the gallery.

Now, at that time there was only one place where top quality eels could be got in Corca Baiscinn and that place was Doolin, not far from Black Head. 'Dubh Linn' in Irish means the black pool and there *was* a pool there, just where the Aille river runs into the sea. In that place the finest of fat eels gathered because

stranger was soon standing before the king's seat in the great hall, where he blurted out his story.

'Your majesty! A terrible thing! Ballykinvarga fort is invaded by villains and they're saying that this year they won't let you bring any eels through their land if you don't pay them a sack full of the purest gold.'

'What!' cried Aengus, jumping up in a fury. 'No eels?'

'No, your majesty,' said the messenger, almost collapsing. He was covered in blood from the fierce hammering he had got. As he was passing about his lawful business the blackguards in Ballykinvarga fort had stopped him, taken him in, beaten him inside with sticks and stones and then let him off to bring back the message to King Aengus that they meant business.

'Oh, your majesty, they're in earnest this time. They said they're sick and tired of letting you and all your people take advantage of them by crossing their lands, and not a penny out of it, so this time they're determined. No gold, no eels.'

'By my father's trousers,' shouted Aengus, and his hand thumped the table, 'they won't get away with this. Call for the Fianna!'

The word went out and soon Fionn was inside before the king discussing this serious problem. He was angry and disgusted. Only the previous day he and twenty of the Fianna had arrived from Tara, specially invited for the May feast. Now it seemed that it might have to be cancelled. Every man there was steaming mad. They took it as an insult to themselves and to the High King also, so it was no surprise when

Fionn, turning to his men, asked, 'What are we going to do?'

'We'll get the eels!' The roar of twenty large voices all at once shook the dust from the rafters, down on Aengus' beard.

'Start going, so,' said he, 'while the house is still standing. And look! Ye have only three days to get the eels, make them fellows see the light of day and get back here in time for the feast, otherwise there's going to be murder. I'll see can I keep the crowd quiet for a while with the pickled eels in the cellars. But hurry! Are ye gone yet?'

'Right, your majesty,' said Fionn. 'You can depend on us to bring them back alive.'

They set out that very hour, all twenty-one of them, armed to the teeth, and soon they were in the Burren. At that time the road to Doolin was far longer than it is now and followed a different course. Due south it stretched from Cathair Mhór to Corkscrew Hill and on to Ballykinvarga, then west from there to the sea. Also at that time the Burren was fine land – in spite of the name (which means 'stony place'). There was very little rock to be seen there so they found the journey no great trial. They got to Corkscrew Hill in record time and were making great progress. Since they were used to long marches of a hundred miles and more in a single day with all their equipment they hardly regarded this as more than a morning's stroll. The road up Corkscrew Hill in those days was very much as it is today, twisting over and back, all the way up. The Fianna were so busy marching, with their heads down, admiring their battle-sandals, that they never saw the sinister figures moving at the top of the hill.

These men had made their preparations carefully: huge rocks lined along the hilltop, each one balanced carefully, ready to roll at the slightest push. The men of Ballykinvarga fort knew King Aengus well and what his strategy would be and so they had laid a trap. They said to themselves, 'Aha! Weren't we right, to think that Aengus wouldn't wait, that he'd send out the heavy lads to move us. But, faith, they can have these instead of eels and see how they like them.'

With that, they rolled the big rocks down on top of Fionn and his men.

Goll was first to hear the RRRRRRumble and feel the ground trembling.

'Mind out, lads!' he roared, panic in his voice. 'Jump out of it!'

They did, and lucky for them, too. Down over ditches, heather and stone walls came the rocks and they would surely have made puddle out of any man unlucky enough to be in their path.

'A Thiarna!' gasped Fionn, ''twas lucky we heard them coming.'

They were just collecting their scattered wits and blowing the dust off themselves when a shower of arrows darkened the sky and rained down on top of them. They raised their shields to make a roof for themselves, and there they crouched waiting for Fionn to decide on their next move.

'Begob, they mean it, whoever they are,' he said, 'but that's no reason why the Fianna are going to take it from them. Come on! Every man, draw his sword, and up the hill with ye! We're afraid of no one, dead or alive!'

They did exactly that. The tracks that the rocks made coming down, the Fianna used going up, and in the space of five minutes they were standing panting on top of the hill. But there was no one there to greet them. The ambushers had seen them coming. No fear they were going to wait for the Fianna! They skipped away through the heather, anxious to put space between themselves and Fionn's men, but pleased too that they had caused annoyance to such famous warriors at no cost to themselves.

Fionn called the men and they stood in a circle around him.

'Now lads, look! We'll have to be careful from here on because these boys are out to make things rough for us. We'll have to go easy and watch where we're putting our legs. There could be all kinds of traps set for us. But remember, too, that we have to get the eels and we have less than three days to do it. So come on!'

They advanced, but far more carefully than before. There was no whistling now or singing as they passed through Baur and Gleann Slaod since they did not want their enemies ahead to know where they were. That night, near the stone fort of Caherconnell, they made their camp. But before they lit their camp fire they were careful to build a large shelter for it from rocks which they quarried especially for the purpose. They did this so that they might avoid being seen from the high ground on every side. Anything they ate that night was eaten cold from the bag and swallowed with water. Then they rested in the shade of the huge stones they had raised. To this very day their refuge stands in that place, Poulnabrone, a wonder to all who come to view it.

The following morning, Fionn said, 'Now, men, today we're going to be getting to the fort, the big stone fort of Ballykinvarga; and the fellows inside there, I'm telling ye they're no joke, and they'll be trying to stop us passing. But what can we do, when our road to Doolin passes outside the walls of it? There's no other way but to pass opposite the gate. So here's what we'll do. I know that fort well, and I know because I was in on the building of it. The story is too long now to be telling ye,' said he, 'but in short, me and my father laid a fair few of them stones.'

'Aw! Tell us the story,' groaned all the Fianna together. Fionn gaped. He could not understand this kind of carry-on at all, but he knew how stubborn they could be when they were disappointed, so he settled his spear and leaned on it.

'When I was a young fellow I was here in this part of the kingdom with my father. We were fighting a giant here at the time, and there was a bet that since we couldn't get the better of each other in battle we'd settle who was the better by a building contest. The one that'd build most and biggest in one night would win the bet and the loser, he'd have to jump off the Cliffs of Moher. Now, my oul' father, he was a fair hand at building so he had no great worry on him. Anyway, two big forts were built that night and the following day when it came to measuring to see who did most work, it turned out that myself and my father had a better job done, so the giant had to take a jump for himself.

91

'Now ye have it all, so shake it up, there! And remember, I know what I'm talking about when I tell ye 'tis a strong fort we're facing. There's no way into it,' said he, 'except one small door, and I'm telling ye there'll be no knocking the walls, so we could be in right trouble. Them fellows, they have no right to be inside in that fort at all – no one should be living in it – but they must have gone in when they saw how strong it was, barred the small door, and faith, we'll have our work cut out for us trying to get them out of it.'

He was just moving off with the rest of the men when a thought came to him and he held up his hand to stop again.

'Now that I think of it, there's one chance, all right,' he thought talking to himself. 'There might be no hope of us breaking it down from outside, but what's to stop us from doing it from the inside?'

The men looked at him.

'Inside? But, sure, aren't we outside and so how can we attack it from the inside? Is there a tunnel, or what?'

Fionn was not pleased to hear this kind of talk.

'Look! Leave the thinking to me or else go home and be shamed.'

That quietened them.

'What we'll do is this,' said Fionn. 'We'll make little of the fellows inside. We'll call them cowards and warts and bandits, all kinds of dirty names like that. But we'll keep well out of the way of their spears and arrows, and if they have any bit of the man in them at all there should be a fine shower of weapons coming out to us as long as we keep up the abuse. But when they have all fired at us, and no way of getting any more we'll abuse their fathers and mothers and grand- fathers, all back along to the start of time, and if that doesn't drive them mad altogether I'm losing my touch. If it works like I think, it won't be long before they'll be throwing the stones out of the wall at us. And ye know what the finish of that will be. So now, every man think of as many dirty names as he can while we're marching.'

They all looked at Fionn with reverence and admira- tion. Oh, how lucky they were to have a man of intel- ligence like him in charge. The clever way he had of doing things! They breathed one big sigh of satis- faction and off they went, every one of them with his eyebrows twisted, thinking up names to throw into the fort.

About five miles farther on, more suddenly than even Fionn expected, a stone battlement loomed up in front of them. They stopped.

'Oh boy!' they said all together in admiration. 'That took building, Fionn. Are you telling us that yourself and your father built it in one night!'

'We did. We did. We had help, of course,' said Fionn. 'I didn't tell ye that part of the story, and we won't talk about it now, either. Ye know the interest- ing bit and that'll do for the moment. Now, up to the fort with three of you!' – he picked three volunteers – 'and give them the message from King Aengus. We have to be fair, whatever else. But if they won't come out tell them we have a job to do and we'll do it.'

The three men advanced, Conán in command. He

stood out, all his armour glittering in the sunlight, and he said to the heads that were appearing above the wall of the fort, 'You men, inside in the fort! I want a word with the leader. Where is he? *Who* is he? Let him show his face and we'll see who he is.'

No sound for a few moments. Then a large head rose up slowly above the wall. Oh, but he was a squinty-eyed old warrior, a fierce, ugly-looking ogre. But he had little height – a kind of dwarf with a humped back and special armour to cover this deformity.

'Dar an leabhar (By the book)!' cried Conán, 'look who's in it. Leathshúil himself!' Conán had had a few twists of swordplay with this ruffian before now so he knew him well. The rumour was that he had been with the fairies but had tried to cheat them of their gold so they fixed his eyes in different directions to put him astray for the future and teach him manners. But it had not worked. It only made him bad-minded and stubborn. And here he was now, so there was trouble in store for everyone.

Out of the corner of his mouth Conán said to his two companions, 'Lads, there's going to be things flying here in a couple of minutes so be ready to move. There's no talking with this boyo. I know him and he's a bad case.'

But he said to Leathshúil in a calm voice, 'I remember you well, Leathshúil. You have no right in that fort, and even if you had you have no business to be blocking King Aengus' eels. You know right well that he wants them for his feast and he must have them! So you'd do well now, my dear man, to step aside and let us pass peacefully, or there'll be trouble.'

In reply Leathshúil gave an evil laugh, 'Hee-hoh-heeee!' a gruesome chortle, then swung down his hand inside the wall. At once a shower of arrows sliced through the air. Conán had been expecting a trick like this and even before Leathshúil had finished cackling the three were skipping their way back to Fionn and the rest of the Fianna, arrows hopping off the rocks on every side of them. There was another blast of cackling from the fort. Fionn shook with temper but he said nothing until Conán and the two men jumped in behind the wall where he was and told him the answer they had got.

"'Tis well I know what he said to ye, but, faith, he'll have a different song this evening.'

He gathered the men around him and said, 'Remember the plan. Out now, with shields in front of ye and make them fire all their arrows. But be careful. I don't want anyone killed so early in the day.'

Out they trooped, but not too close to the fort. They did not need to be told by Fionn to mind themselves! They came forward to where a low stone wall snaked along the level ground in front of the fort and stood behind it with their shields up.

The whole battlements of the fort were lined with men now, every one of them firing arrows out as fast as he could load. But it never dawned on them that this was what Fionn wanted, nor did they stop to think why no arrows were coming back against them or why the Fianna came no farther than the low stone wall. The first hint they had that anything was wrong was when they began to put back their hands for arrows. . . only to find their quivers empty. They were out of ammunition!

The Fianna, behind their wall, noticed the shower of arrows lightening. . . lightening. . . then stopping.

'Ha-hah!' laughed Fionn, 'they must have them all used. The second part of the plan, men. Now!'

All together, they jumped out over the wall, put down their spears and shields and started picking their nails with their daggers – a mortal insult to the men in the fort –, making faces and calling out most fierce and horrible jeers.

Those inside were stupefied. Never had they been taunted like this before! But the insults were not finished yet. Putting aside even their daggers, the men of the Fianna started a céilí beneath the walls, Goll and Feardorcha providing the puss-music. Every time a chorus came up they all began to mock Leath-shúil and his men, saying that what they badly needed for the dancing were partners, and would the dear ladies inside be kind enough to join them, 'Ha-haw-hawww-hawwwwwwww!'

An evil fog of temper rose over the wall of the fort. Leathshúil by now was gnawing the handle of his sword and leaving toothprints on the rocks at the top of the wall by dint of pure badness.

Fionn, in spite of all his dancing, was keeping a close eye on the fort, but there was no sign yet that those inside were about to make any move to start part three of his plan.

'We'll have to give them a bit of encouragement,' he nodded to Goll. 'Look at this stone wall here! Throw a few wallopers of rocks out of it at them and that might give them the idea.'

Some of the men kept the céili going while the rest began to throw stones from the wall. Nice, handy-sized boulders they were too, about the weight of a man, but no bother at all to big strong men like the Fianna, men who were accustomed to casting from the time they were in the cradle. Leathshúil was still grinding away on the wall when one of these flying monsters landed on his cranium. Lucky for him he was wearing his helmet. The back of his head escaped injury; but his teeth were not so lucky. Now instead of his toothprints on the stone, his entire set of fangs were embedded.

When his men saw him go under their courage vanished and they rushed headlong off the wall as rocks continued to sail in over it, crashing off one another and rising sparks all around them. They huddled into one corner looking helpless and stupid, but luckily for them Leathshúil pried his face free, got his voice and roared: 'Ye crowd of gamalls (louts)! Are ye going to stand there like a herd of cows and let that crowd outside flatten ye? Scatter out and start sending back some of them rocks to Fionn Mac Cumhail.'

They leaped to obey, and so the battle started in earnest. Now that Leathshúil was again in command the men inside were soon giving as good as they got so that the Fianna had to move back when they had all their own ammunition thrown into the fort. Fionn quickly saw that his plan was not going as he had hoped. The Fianna were supposed to let the lads in the fort do *all* the pelting, not match them rock for rock!

'Slow down, men! Easy! Easy!' he shouted, but he might as well have been talking to the wall – if it had still been there! The Fianna were scattering in every direction, looking for boulders of all sizes to fling in on their enemies. Worst of all was that the men were enjoying themselves highly so Fionn knew he would have to scrap this part of his plan and think of something else, and quickly.

As the men staggered back, warping under huge loads of limestone, Fionn stopped each in turn, made him pile all his ammunition in one big heap and go off for more. It went on like this until they had a nice-sized hill of rocks ready. Fionn called them together then.

'Ten men will do the throwing, and the rest of ye keep collecting. Go on!'

They did that. And all the while, over their shoulders, they could hear the groaning and straining, trousers tearing and buttons popping in the fort as men strove to lift huge but unseen weights.

'They're up to the very same trick as ourselves,' said the men gleefully as they tried ever harder.

'The best throwing-arms are going to win this battle,' said Fionn, 'but it won't be won without more rocks, either.'

Those gathering set off on a circuit of miles around the country collecting big chunks of rock. Any place they saw one they tore it out of the ground, 'Grrrhhn,' pulling it up like a bulldozer would today. Then back it was brought to Fionn who broke it at once with his bare hands and threw it on the heap.

When there was enough in the heap for a few solid

hours' fighting the gatherers rested and Fionn gave the order to fire, and a curtain of stone swept towards the fort. But it was met half-way by a hail of rock on the way out and the splinters began to land like hailstones all around. The sky grew dark from the whizzing to and fro of rocks and dust, and at the height of the battle one side scarcely was able to see what the other was doing. It was lucky for all that the flying missiles made such a wind that the dust was blown away. But that same cloud darkened all the land of Corca Baiscinn for two weeks and as it spread the people for miles around knew that a terrible fight was in progress.

On and on it went, to and fro, in and out, until night came on that second day. The Fianna were tired, but so were the defenders of the fort. All of their hands were nearly pulled off from the throwing, carting and dragging of rocks from all angles.

If the effect of the day's work on sinew and muscle was severe, on the landscape it was far worse. As far as the eye could see it was all rooted up because by now they were having to travel further and burrow deeper in order to find suitable ammunition. Nowhere was safe from their prying fingers, and what a strange-looking lunar country it was by the time they finished their day's fighting.

That night Fionn sat by his camp-fire, his hands stretched out to the heat, and thought about the following day.

'Tomorrow, men, there's going to be a long day in it, and wicked fighting. And tomorrow we're going to have to take that place because we have only one day

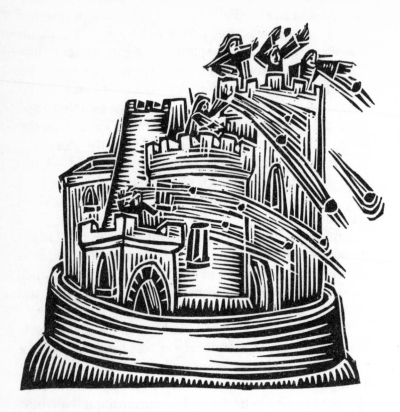

left now to get the eels for King Aengus, and we can't spend all that time trying to teach manners to this gang.'

'What can we do, though?' asked Goll in an exhausted voice. 'They have no notion of giving up or coming out.'

'Well I know it,' replied Fionn. 'But I have something here that might make our job a small bit easier.'

From his pack he pulled a tightly-wrapped bundle

100

and unwrapped it. There lay a yellow mass of a sticky-looking substance somewhat like butter.

'But isn't that the stuff we rub on the axles of the chariots?'

They began to look at him as though he, rather than Leathshúil, had been hit on the head.

'It is and it isn't,' he answered mysteriously. 'Ask no questions now, only rub that to your arms tonight, and tomorrow they'll be as good as new. So Taoscán told me when I asked him for something to help us.'

At the mention of the chief druid's name their doubts vanished. Each man applied the yellow mess to his arms without more protest. And so they slept.

The following morning dawned and Fionn woke with a pain throbbing in his fighting-arm. He, being the leader, had not been able to avail of the arm-fixer so he had to make the best of it. But then he reminded himself of the inmates of Ballykinvarga and how they must be feeling without any arm-fixer, and the life began to ebb back into his arm again. He rose and issued his instructions: 'Today, the men that were throwing yesterday will change over and do the root-ing and carrying for a change. That way we'll be able to give a better account of ourselves.'

When the rooters were gone off Fionn cocked his ear at the fort. Not a sound!

'Heh,' said he, 'the lazy sots! But we'll wake them up. 'Tis a pity to have this fine hill of limestone idle here and the day passing. Here's what we'll do. All of us that are here, we'll throw these in on top of them, all together, and begob, we'll bury the fort. If we work it with the two hands they'll never know what hit them.'

They set to it. Every man caught hold of a jagged rock, and what an inspiring sight it was to see them, balancing and fingering, getting the best grip for a good accurate throw. Anyone watching them would have recognised that they were experts at it.

'Right,' said Fionn. 'When I give the word!'

There was no sound for a few seconds except for a thrush singing and a hedgehog rustling somewhere in a ditch.

'Go!'

Up strained the hands, all together, and SHWWSHhhh, in over the wall of the fort went the early-morning waker-uppers. SKRSSHH! KRNNSSHHH!!

Bombs from the air could have come as no greater surprise than this rough present first thing in the morning. A grey cloud of dust rose from inside and a few screeches, as part of the big wall collapsed under the weight of the tons of rocks from the Fianna.

Silence fell for a minute. But then, out from behind the battered wall came a scatter of the boulders that had sailed in a short time before, some of them with pieces of the men they fell on still stuck to them.

'Run, lads!' yelled Fionn, and they scattered, because CRASH! BANG! down came the rocks among them.

On the battle went, pounding, pelting, fighting and tearing, with missiles flying in all directions. Towards noon Fionn said, 'Lads, my courage is failing me. There's only one way of finishing this in time. Everyone, throw! No more collecting! Throw double quick, two hands! Something'll surely have to give here soon on one side or the other.'

He was obeyed at once. The men were like windmills now, their hands whirling around. A hill of rocks was never shifted as fast as they shifted that one. For a time it looked as if all would not do, though, because the barrage of rocks from inside the fort seemed as strong as ever. But Fionn noticed, about three o'clock, that those inside were not as accurate as they had been at the start. The trouble was that neither were the Fianna, because by this time finger-tips were becoming flittered and frayed. Two days' hard work with Clare stone was beginning to tell

'We're going to lose this battle with time, men,' groaned Fionn when he saw with dismay that as many rocks were missing the fort as hitting it.

'We'll have to think of something new. And fast!'

He thought for a second. Then, 'Aha!' said he. 'I have it! I hate doing this but we're running out of time and Aengus must have his eels.'

He reached his hand into his oxter-bag and pulled out the first thing that came to his fingers, a squat dark bottle.

'What's in this, I wonder?' he said. It was completely without markings.

'Open it up there, quick,' said Conán, 'and we'll see.'

Fionn pulled out the cork with his teeth and sniffed it. No smell at all! He poured a drop of it out on his hand and immediately hair began to sprout on his palm.

'Oh, a thiarna, 'tis fierce powerful stuff,' he gasped. 'Here! Take a steall (gulp) of it, Goll, and tell us what 'tis like. . . if you're able.'

Goll hesitated, looked around him as if he felt he might be looking at his friends for the last time.

'Well? What's your delay?' shouted Fionn. 'Is it so you think I'd try to poison you?'

Goll took the bottle slowly and they all stood gaping with their mouths open, watching him, while he drank it down. No sooner had the liquid touched his tongue than his eyes popped open, his hair stood up on end and he let out a screech.

'Let me at them! I'll finish them myself.'

He was as fresh as a daisy again, mad for a fight. All the tiredness was gone out of him in a second and his fingers were as good as new. The rest of the men needed no more proof.

'Give us the bottle, quick!' demanded Fionn, snatching it from Goll, fearful that it might be broken.

'Pass it on, will ye!' snapped someone else. Everyone had his hand in there and sooner or later everyone got a drop of this strong stuff, whatever it was. Conán Maol was keeping a watchful eye out for an extra drop to rub to his bald head but by the time the bottle came round to him again it was dry. Every drop was drained. He might have cried there and then, but Fionn left no time for that. He rammed the bottle back into the oxter-bag and turned to look at the men. Oh, what a difference from the poor specimens they had been five minutes before! They were jumping out of their skins now with energy, mad for any kind of action.

'No excuse for any man not doing a gaisce (mighty deed) now,' Fionn chortled. 'Double fire with every hand ye have! I want that fort buried in the time I'm smoking my pipe.'

If they were like windmills before, even a poet would be hard put to describe them now, so hard did they bend themselves to it. In twenty minutes every stone for six miles around was flung in on top of the fort, and Goll and Conán were so full of life that they were even talking about opening up a new quarry in Liscannor to slate it. There was no need. The rocks coming out of the fort dwindled to nothing and by the time Fionn had cleaned and put away his pipe there was no fort at all to be seen. It was buried.

A dead quietness spread over the land. The dust settled and when it did Fionn and his men gathered up their weapons, walked to where the fort had been and surveyed the mound, no word out of anyone. They listened intently for a while. Then they sent the dogs up along the stones to find whether they could smell anyone stirring. Not a movement. Those inside were there to stay.

'Heh! Heh!' laughed Fionn. 'The only way they'll see the light of day now is to burrow their way out, like a herd of rabbits. They were so fond of the place, they can have it all to themselves. I'd say we'll be safe enough now. But just to make double sure we'll leave ten of ye here to keep guard, and as soon as any of them lads puts out his head – if any of them do – grab a hold of him and tie him up. Threaten him that ye'll shorten his neck if he has any noise out of him. Now! Off to Doolin with the rest of us! Them eels must be brought today.'

They set off, trotting, and they got to Doolin in double quick time with no more trouble. All along the road they were whistling again, joking and laughing to one another: 'Oh, Aengus'll be delighted with the job we did.'

'Will we get an extra feed of eels for it, I wonder?' and so on.

When they arrived at Doolin they found out that the eels were all loaded up and ready, packed in big timber kegs, full of water so that they would be alive and snapping when they arrived at Aengus' kitchen. Only the cats would benefit if they arrived dead. Even cooks as good as those of Aengus could be expected to do only so much, after all.

But there was a problem, as they found out after a short while in Doolin. The horses that were provided to pull the big carts laden with the barrels were gone. They had been stolen by the evil robbers of Crusheen the night before and carried off into the wilds of Doire Olc.

'That's what the delay at the fort did to us, now,' said Conán. 'You could trust no one these days!'

'Well, the devil take them,' snarled Fionn. 'But we have no time to be going into that wild place now after those thieves. We have less than a day to get this cargo back to Aengus, because the cooks'll need time to get working on them to have everything ready for the feast. There's nothing else for it but to pull these carts ourselves. So come on! The whole lot of ye! Load up the weapons and ye can be the horses.'

What else could they do? Under the shafts of the carts they went and began to pull on the hard road for home. Of course, Fionn's rank as leader did not allow him to do so. He was in front, giving orders: 'Come on, there! Hi-hi! Conán, you're slowing up. Pick up your hind legs there.' In spite of any misgivings they might have felt they made the road fly under them. On past Carnaun, Slievenabillogue, Ballykeel, and when they arrived back at Ballykinvarga fort the ten men were there yet, doing nothing.

'Stop now! Take a rest,' Fionn ordered the men under the shafts, and he approached the ten guards.

'Well? Any noise out of the boys inside?'

'Not a geek,' replied one of the guards.

'That's great. We'll leave them there, to hell. Now, the ten of you are after a fine rest, so come on! Ye can take a turn under the shafts.'

The guards swapped places with the ten who had pulled from Doolin and off they all galloped again. They made speedy progress – until they came to Corkscrew Hill. That was where the fun started! As the first two men cantered down the hill the carts began to run away with them. The road was so steep and the barrels of eels were so heavy that even strong men like the Fianna could not hold them back. They nearly burst themselves trying to stop, and the soles and hobnails were torn off their sandals as they skidded faster and faster down the hill.

'Stop! Stop!' howled Fionn. 'Run the shafts into the wall till we think of a way of getting down this cursed place in one piece!'

He need not have spoken. Already that solution had suggested itself to the men and one by one they jolted to a halt. Luckily they were all expert chariot-drivers and well used to dangerous driving, so not an eel was spilt. Now, balancing the shafts of the carts on the

108

stone walls, they struggled out and gathered into a huddle in the middle of the road.

'The only way I can see of doing it,' said Fionn, 'is the hard way. Each of us'll have to catch a hold of one of the carts, take off the barrels and the wheels, and take it down on his back.'

Which they did. One by one, they brought down carts, barrels and wheels, until all was transported to the level ground. But three hours had been lost in doing so and another thirty minutes in getting tackled up and ready for the road again. When that was done Fionn said breathlessly, 'Next ten. men under the shafts and let out the first ten! Quick! Look at the way the sun is' – he was keeping a close eye to the sky – 'we have only a few hours left to get the eels back, or Aengus'll have a seizure, and we'll have no feast, which is a lot worse.'

He knew now that there was only one way to get more speed out of them so he set them to race each other.

'Come on! Run! Run! The road is level from here on. Keep going! An extra plate of jellied eels to the man first home! We have over four miles to go yet, so 'tis anyone's race.'

People rushed out of their houses along the way to see the sight. The Rás Tailteann was nothing compared to it. Sweat flowed off them as freely as Torc Waterfall, spattering and wetting spectators standing at the side of the road, and the RRUUMMBLL! RUMMMBLL! of the big wheels and the barrels going splish-splash! Splish-splash! above made music as they raced along.

It was dark by the time they approached Cathair Mhór, Aengus' fort, and Aengus himself was on the battlements stamping over and back, over and back, temper written in every wrinkle of his face.

'Gnnh! Where are my eels? Where *are* my eels?'

Then one of the guards ran up, breathless, and wheezed, 'Your majesty, there's noise coming the road. Would it be your eels, do you think?'

'Hurra, it had *better* be my eels or there'll be noise here. I'll take the heads off Fionn Mac Cumhail and the rest of them.'

He waited five minutes. Ten minutes. The noise along the road got louder, louder, until. . . out of the gloom the first of the carts came in sight. When Aengus saw that he sent out servants immediately with torches, to guide them in. When he saw who was under the shafts of the carts, that there was no horse there at all, he burst out into big scairts (guffaws) of laughter. He forgot entirely how angry, how vicious he had been only a few minutes before, and while the Fianna thundered into the courtyard with their loads he remained above, bursting his buttons laughing at them.

Then he came down.

'Ye're a fine-looking bunch of horses, there's no doubt about it. You know, I might change my policy in future altogether and hire horses for my army and keep ye for my stables instead. Hee! hee!'

Fionn saw no humour in that at all, but he was only too accustomed to kings and their little jokes so he said nothing. The men under the carts had nothing to say either; they were bathed in a lather of sweat.

111

All they could do was lie down in a corner and fall asleep immediately, steam rising from the tattered remnants of their sandals. Only burned skin and frayed toenails now remained.

When Aengus saw that his joke was received with stony silence he became almost embarrassed and went off about his business, leaving Fionn to see to the comfort of his men as best he could.

Now the cooks took charge of the barrels, emptied the water and carried the eels to the kitchens to begin working on them. They fried, boiled, toasted, roasted and frittered; they made pastes and pastries, all kinds of pies and what-not. And oh, the difference in two or three hours! A reek of cooking eels spread to all corners of the fort, but no one minded that. Quite the opposite – it merely gave them more of an appetite for the feed to come.

Everything was ready on time. All the tables were laid, perfect in every detail, and when the guests surged into the feasting-hall not one of them guessed what trouble those eels had caused. But the problems were not half over, though no one yet knew that.

The feast went off beautifully, of course, but none of the Fianna was there except Fionn, and people noticed this because, as one man said, 'Weren't the men of the Fianna specially invited? Wouldn't you think they'd show a bit of courtesy to our beloved king, and come when they're asked.' Aengus could throw no light on the mystery. Fionn, even though he could have, didn't. He it was who had picked them out of the corner where they fell in a dead heap and carried them, every one, upstairs to the big guests' bedroom of the fort and left them all lying in the one big bed, sound asleep. There they lay now, and for three days afterwards, dead to the world and shaking the walls with their snoring.

From that day on, if the word eel was mentioned to those men they would attack and skin the person who had been foolish enough to bring up the subject. Never again did they want to see or hear of an eel, either dead or alive.

But back at Cathair Mhór trouble was brewing. For three days after the feast not a sound was to be heard around the fort, not even a dog scratching himself. Every living creature inside was asleep, dreaming about eels and next year's feast. But early on the morning of the fourth day a mob of people gathered at the front gate of the palace and began a fierce hulabaloo. They woke everyone inside with their banging and shouting, even King Aengus, who had eaten a bigger feed of eels than was good for him. He tottered out on to his balcony, scratching his person, loosening his belt and muttering to himself in a low drone. Imagine his amazement when he got to the top step; he had to wipe his eyes to make sure he was seeing correctly. Never had he seen so big a crowd since the day of his coronation at Magh Adhair. All his sleepiness left him in an instant, and his shrewd eye noted that they were farmers. The tools and weapons they brandished made that much quite clear.

When they saw him they shouted, 'We're from the Burren! Do you know what those vandals of yours did, the Fianna? Did you see our fields after them? You couldn't graze a snipe in them now. They destroyed our land; they rooted it all up!'

'They did?' returned Aengus innocently. 'I heard nothing about it if they did.' Then more threateningly, 'Rubbish! Nonsense! Ye're talking ráiméis (rubbish) and I'd advise ye to go home, at once.'

'Home, is it?' they roared. 'Do you expect us to live under stones? Come up and see it for yourself.'

'D'ye think I have nothing better to be doing besides walking my lands at this hour of the day?' demanded Aengus, getting very red in the face.

But there was no quietening that crowd. They threatened to pay no more rent unless something was done to answer their grievances, so he told them to wait, that he would question Fionn. Fionn was summoned to the royal presence.

'What's this I hear from that gang out there? They're saying you ruined the land on them, that 'tis only full of stones and rocks now, as well as big holes. Is that true?'

''Tis a lie!' shouted Fionn. 'There isn't a rock in it. Sure, didn't we run short of them early on in the battle. I'd never fight in a place like that again.'

But Fionn knew full well what the trouble was. To make matters worse Aengus was looking him straight in the eye, in a very knowing manner. Fionn reconsidered, hesitantly.

'Dhera, sure, look! We had to do a bit of rooting and tunnelling all right to – ah – kind of quieten the crowd inside in Ballykinvarga fort.'

'Ye had?' mused Aengus, walking to and fro, hands folded behind him. 'Well, well! This could be very troublesome, you know. Even expensive. I have no money to be throwing into holes in the Burren at this moment.'

He stopped, turned to Fionn, and his right forefinger jabbed the air.

'D'you know what you'll do? Root up your men out of the bed and tell them there's a small bit of a job in front of them.'

Fionn groaned silently, but he knew what had to be done.

'I'll do that,' he murmured and off he went. Aengus strolled back to the farmers and announced, 'Look! Fionn Mac Cumhail and the Fianna, they'll be up tomorrow to fix up any damage. That's the best I can do for ye because I have no gold in my strong-room at the moment to give ye instead.'

They had to take his word for it and go home. Aengus went back to bed and later that day Fionn and the men tightened their belts and started out, a full day early. They came as far as Ballykinvarga fort, listened closely, but could hear no sound from under the huge mound. So they began to take the rocks again which they had so recently thrown in on top of the fort, and hurled them out in every direction, out around the countryside until the fort could be seen once more. They walked among the ruins then and found many men inside, flattened. But of Leathshúil there was no trace.

'Where is that devil gone?' said Conán.

'He had some gruagach (goblin) protecting him, surely,' muttered Fionn, rubbing his chin with his thumb.

If the farmers had cause to complain about the state

of their land before this, they nearly lost their lives altogether when they saw it now. But Fionn and the men at the fort knew nothing about this. They were delighted with their day's exercise and when they looked about them Feardorcha Mac Fichill even said, 'This is a fine burren of a place now. I'll bet any one of ye that people will come from the four corners of the world to see the grand job we did here this day.'

He was right about that.

But the farmers, when they saw what the Fianna had done, were tearing their hair with temper.

'Aaaa! Yeee! Blast it, sure the land is useless now. Look at the cut of it! There's no soil in it at all, only a solid sheet of rock.'

Back they went to Cathair Mhór again, an evil-tempered mob, armed with pikes and other weapons. But this time Aengus was wide awake and had no intention of even seeing them at first. At last, under pressure from his advisers, he came out on the balcony, a scowl on his face, his hands clenched behind his back – a sure sign that he was in a bad humour.

'Get out of here at once, or I'll set the dogs and the Fianna on ye. Ye weren't satisfied the first time and now, when the job is done right, ye aren't satisfied either. So be going, while ye can.' And he stalked off.

What else could they do but slink away, back to their ruined fields? Eventually they had to leave that part of Clare entirely because they could get no living from it any more. Anyone who looks at the Burren today will understand why, for it remains yet just as the Fianna left it all those centuries ago.

TALES OF IRISH ENCHANTMENT
Patricia Lynch

Patricia Lynch brings to this selection of classical Irish folktales for young people all the imagination and warmth for which she is renowned.

There are seven stories here: Midir and Etain, The Quest of the Sons of Turenn, The Swan Children, Deirdre and the Sons of Usna, Labra the Mariner, Cuchulain – The Champion of Ireland and The Voyage of Maeldun.

They lose none of their original appeal in the retelling and are as delightful today as when they were first told.

The stories are greatly enhanced by the immediacy and strength of Frances Boland's imaginative drawings.

ENCHANTED IRISH TALES
Patricia Lynch

Enchanted Irish Tales tells of ancient heroes and heroines, fantastic deeds of bravery, magical kingdoms, weird and wonderful animals... This new illustrated edition of classical folktales, retold by Patricia Lynch with all the imagination and warmth for which she is renowned, rekindles the age-old legends of Ireland, as exciting today as they were when first told. The collection includes:

- Conary Mór and the Three Red Riders
- The Long Life of Tuan Mac Carrell
- Finn Mac Cool and Fianna
- Oisin and The Land of Youth
- The Kingdom of The Dwarfs
- The Dragon Ring of Connla
- Mac Datho's Boar
- Ethne

IRISH FAIRY TALES
Michael Scott

'He found he was staring directly at a leprechaun. The small man was sitting on a little mound of earth beneath the shade of a weeping willow tree... The young man could feel his heart beginning to pound. He had seen leprechauns a few times before but only from a distance. They were very hard to catch, but if you managed at all to get hold of one...'

Michael Scott's exciting stories capture all the magic and mystery of Irish folklore. This collection of twelve fairy tales, beautifully and unusually illustrated, include:

The arrival of the Tuatha de Danann in Erin

The fairy horses	The King's secret
The crow goddess	The fairies' revenge
The wise woman's payment	The shoemaker and himself
The floating island	The sunken town

IRISH ANIMAL TALES
Michael Scott

'Have you ever noticed how cats and dogs sometimes sit up and look at something that is not there? Have you ever seen a dog barking at nothing? And have you ever wondered why? Perhaps it is because the animals can see the fairy folk coming and going all the time, while humans can only see the little People at certain times...'

This illustrated collection of Michael Scott's strange stories reveal a wealth of magical creatures that inhabit Ireland's enchanted animal kingdom. The tales tell of the king of the cats, the magical cows, the fox and the hedgehog, the dog and the leprechaun, March, April and the Brindled Cow, the cricket's tale... A collection to entrance readers, both young and old.

Stories of Old Ireland for Children

Eddie Lenihan

Long ago in Ireland there were men who used to travel to the four corners of the earth and few travelled farther than Fionn and the men of the Fianna during their many exciting adventures. In *Stories of Old Ireland for Children* we read about 'Fionn MacCumhail and the Feathers from China', 'King Cormac's Fighting Academy' and 'Fionn and the Mermaids'.

A Spooky Irish Tale for Children

Eddie Lenihan

Before the coming of a dark stranger from Thurginia in Germany, pictures had never been painted in Ireland. The artist is welcomed even in the royal palace of Tara, where he decorates the walls of every room. But in return for this amazing new craft a high price is demanded: a series of gruesome killings that are carried out within the royal palace itself. Taoscán Mac Liath, the high king's chief druid and the wisest man in the land is puzzled, but he finds out enough to realise that if something is not done – and quickly – there will be few people left to enjoy the beautiful paintings. He enlists the help of Fionn Mac Cumhail to solve the eerie and terrible mystery.

FIONN MACCUMHAIL AND THE BAKING HAGS

Edmund Lenihan

Fionn MacCumhail and his companions might manage the usual run of everyday terrors – dragons, giants, monster moths and such – but they had precious little answer to the forces of the Dark. For this they had to rely on the knowledge and skills of the druids, especially the High King's own druid, Taoscán MacLiath.

But will he be powerful enough when the wrath of the terrible sisters, Adahbh and Eibhliú, the baking hags, is drawn down on the people of Ireland by a careless error during the building of the new royal highway to the west? It appears that even Taoscán's power may not be enough.